D0046378

GOSHEN PUBLIC LIBRARY
601 SOUTH FIFTH STREET
GOSHEN, IN 46526-3994
DISCARDED
Goshen Public Library

SURPRISE PARTY

Also by Marilyn Sachs

Another Day

Ghosts in the Family

Thirteen Going on Seven

What My Sister Remembered

Circles

At the Sound of the Beep

Just Like a Friend

Matt's Mitt & Fleet-Footed Florence

Fran Ellen's House

Almost Fifteen

Baby Sister

Underdog

Thunderbird

The Fat Girl

Fourteen

Beach Towels

Call Me Ruth

DISCARDED
Goshen Public Librar

GOSHEN PUBLIC LIBRARY
601 SOUTH FIFTH STREET
GOSHEN, IN 46526-3994

Marilyn Sachs

Dutton Children's Books
New York

SAC

Copyright © 1998 by Marilyn Sachs
All rights reserved. No part of this publication may be reproduced or
transmitted in any form or by any means, electronic or mechanical, including
photocopy, recording, or any information storage and retrieval system now
known or to be invented, without permission in writing from the publisher,
except by a reviewer who wishes to quote brief passages in connection with
a review written for inclusion in a magazine, newspaper, or broadcast.

CIP Data is available.

Published in the United States by Dutton Children's Books,
a member of Penguin Putnam Inc.
375 Hudson Street, New York, New York 10014
Designed by Ellen M. Lucaire
Printed in USA
First Edition
ISBN 0-525-45962-6
3 5 7 9 10 8 6 4 2

For my enchanting, irresistible granddaughter, Sarah,
with many oooo's and xxxxx's

SURPRISE PARTY

CHAPTER ONE

▪▪▪▪▪

Genevieve Bishop did not exactly hate her brother.

She didn't want him to be hit by an out-of-control truck, or die from a lingering illness, or disappear in an explosion. Nothing like that. Most of the time, she wasn't even sorry he had been born. She just wished that he had been born into another family.

That was the way she usually felt. But on the day he dangled her little glass slipper out of her bedroom window, she would have been content with any of the above.

"I'll kill you," she shrieked at him. "I'll break every bone in your body. I'll tell Mom. I'll tell Dad. Give it back, you lousy brat!"

He stood there, all powerful, his meanest, broadest grin stretching across his nasty little face.

She considered tackling him and wrestling the slipper away, but he must have understood what she had in mind, because he gave it a little tap on the outside window ledge.

"Don't come any closer," he said, "or I'll let go."

"Ernest," she said solemnly. Maybe solemn would work better than hysterical. "That is a family heirloom. It is very old. It belonged to Grandmother Perl, and then to Mom, and now to me. It has been passed down from generation to generation and is very precious."

Which she knew wasn't really all true. According to Mom, the little glass slipper once was filled with inexpensive candy. Lots of girls Grandmother's age had one, ate the candy, and generally didn't bother saving the glass slipper. But Grandmother Perl did. It was one of the few things Gen knew about Grandmother Perl, mysterious Grandmother Perl. She had owned the little glass slipper when she was a girl, had passed it on to Mom, and now it belonged to Gen.

"Mom gave it to me when I was ten," she said solemnly, "and, one day in the future, I'll pass it on to my own daughter when she turns ten."

"Maybe you won't have a daughter," Ernest said. "Maybe you'll have a son—like me."

I'll kill myself if I do, Gen thought to herself, edging

a little closer. Suddenly it occurred to her that Ernest might be jealous, so she remarked kindly, "Dad's going to give you his beautiful silver pocket knife when you're older. It's a real beauty. I just love that knife."

"Big deal!" Ernest said. "It's all rusty, and one of the blades is broken." He gave the slipper another little tap.

"Stop it!" She resumed screaming. "It's glass. You're going to break it."

"No, it's not glass," Ernest said. "It's plastic. It won't break. Even if I drop it, I bet you it won't break. It's plastic."

"Stupid!" she yelled. "They didn't have plastic when Grandmother Perl was a little girl. That was back in the thirties. It's glass."

"No, it's plastic," Ernest insisted. "Look, I just banged it on the sill, and nothing happened."

"Ernest!"

"See, I just gave it another bang. You don't know everything, Gen. See . . . oh . . . Oh! . . . I guess it was glass."

"Why?" Mom demanded. "Why? I just want to know why you had to destroy something you knew was so precious to your sister."

Gen continued to weep noisily.

"I'm talking to you, Ernest."

"I thought it was plastic."

"But your sister told you it was glass. Didn't she?"

"Yes, but she doesn't know everything. And she never let me hold it, and she kept it locked up in her desk most of the time."

"Well, you certainly can't blame her, can you, after what you did. Now you'd better say you're sorry. Right now!"

"I'm sorry," Ernest said, not looking sorry.

"A lot of good that's going to do me," Gen cried.

"And I think you'll have to replace the glass slipper, won't you?" Mom said.

"You can't replace it," Gen moaned. "They don't make that kind of slipper anymore."

"That's true," Mom said, "but I think if Ernest goes without his allowance for a month . . ."

"Big deal!" Gen said. "That's only four dollars. What can I buy with four dollars?"

"It's the principle," Mom said. "Ernest will go without his allowance for a month, and—let me think a minute. What can he give you to make up for the glass slipper?"

"Nothing," Gen wept. "I loved that slipper more than anything I ever had or ever will have."

"There must be something he has," Mom insisted. "Just think a minute, Gen. There must be something."

"I know." Ernest grinned—the mean grin—the one that spread all across his nasty face. "She can have Dad's old pocket knife."

CHAPTER TWO

■ ■ ■ ■ ■

Dad always insisted that there wasn't a mean bone in all of Ernest's body.

"He didn't mean to break your little glass slipper. He was just curious."

Dad had just returned from work and was trying to hang his jacket up in the closet. Gen had been lying in wait for him.

"That's easy for you to say," she told him. "It wasn't anything precious that belonged to you. I remember when he took your watch apart. You weren't so understanding then."

Dad nodded. "No, I wasn't, and I'm not saying you have to be understanding all the time with him, but . . ."

"And Mom yelled her head off when he broke her music box."

"He's not really mean," Dad said weakly. "Not really mean. He's just . . ."

"Right—just curious. I'm curious too, Dad, but I don't go around breaking things that belong to other people, or making trouble in school, or dropping paper bags filled with water down on people's heads."

"That was because of that kid, Jackie Kohler, who put him up to it. He's a bad influence on Ernest."

"No, Dad, it's the other way around. Ernest is a bad influence on Jackie Kohler and a bad influence on the kids in his class, too."

Dad smiled. "Believe me," he said. "He'll change. You'll see. Anyway, I'm sorry about the little glass slipper. I know it meant a lot to you."

Gen sniffed.

"But maybe Mom and I can think of something to make it up to you."

"You can't," Gen told him. "They don't make them anymore." But she didn't resist when Dad pulled her over to him and gave her a hug.

"So how was my president's big day? How many peasants did you have beheaded?"

Gen couldn't help giggling. She knew Dad was proud of her being president of her class, even though he kept making jokes about it.

"Not as many as I'd like," Gen told him. "There's this kid in my class, Karen Knipper, who's always bad-mouthing me."

"I bet she's jealous," Dad said.

"Anyway, she's a real pain, but today the student council decided that we should send a delegation to the superintendent of schools, asking him to lower class size in the fifth and sixth grades. And Dad, my teacher, Mr. Robbins, asked me to help organize the science fair at school this year, and then I'm definitely going to be on the honor roll again, and I'm working with the calligraphy club to design a new certificate."

"Another slow day at the office," Dad said proudly. He looked happy as he turned toward the closet. "Where's Ernest?" he asked.

"Oh, yes," Gen said. "There's another note from his teacher."

"Oh, no. Not again," Dad said. "Now what?"

Gen brought him the note, and he read it while she waited. He still hadn't been able to hang up his jacket.

"I'm going to have to talk to him," Dad said unhappily. But then he brightened. "Unless your mother did already."

"She went shopping for dinner. Ernest said he forgot to show the note to her before she left, but that was because he knew she was still angry with him over the glass slipper. He's inside watching TV. What does the note say?"

Dad handed her the note and finally hung up his jacket while she read it.

> Dear Mr. & Mrs. Bishop,
>   I'm sorry to say that Ernest continues to disrupt the class. He is forever speaking out of turn when he's not supposed to. He makes funny sounds and tells rude jokes that divert the other students from their work and make them laugh. I would appreciate your cooperation, or I will have to consult with the principal.
>
>   Sincerely,
>   Rosa Chu

"What are you going to do, Dad?" Gen asked, following him into the living room. She always hoped that Dad would blow up and really punish Ernest. In general, it was Mom who lost her temper—Dad seldom did.

"Turn off that set," Dad ordered Ernest in his idea of a scary voice. Gen was disappointed.

"The inning's nearly over," Ernest said.

"Did you hear what I said?" Dad continued in his phony scary voice.

"Pow!" Ernest said, as somebody hit a ball.

Dad strode over to the set and turned it off. "All right, Ernest," he said. "I want an explanation."

Ernest turned his innocent look on Dad. He opened his big blue eyes very wide and shook his curly blond head. "Of what, Dad?"

"You know very well, young man. Ms. Chu says you keep distracting the other kids in the class and making them laugh. Why do you do it?"

"She's boring," Ernest said.

"I don't care what she is. She's your teacher, and you have to respect your teacher and behave in class."

"I didn't say much. Just that there was a cootie crawling up her leg."

"Ernest!" Dad thundered, or tried to thunder. "I want you to promise that from now on, you will stop speaking out of turn, stop making funny noises, and stop telling rude jokes. From now on, I want you to promise that you will speak only when Ms. Chu calls on you."

"She never calls on me."

"Did you hear what I said, Ernest? I want you to say, 'I promise not to speak out of turn or make silly noises, and to stop telling rude jokes. I will speak out only if my teacher calls on me.'"

Dad reached over, grabbed Ernest's arm, and pulled him over to where they could look each other in the eye. Now Gen was impressed. Dad looked almost as if he meant it. But then he blinked first. "I'm talking to you, Ernest. I want you to say 'I promise not to . . .'"

"Okay, okay, I promise," Ernest said. "Now can I watch the game?"

The next day, a note was delivered to Gen's sixth-grade class.

*Please send Genevieve Bishop down
to Ms. Chu's class immediately!*

She was sorry to leave her class because it was club time, and since she belonged to three clubs—the science club, the cooking club, and the calligraphy club—she already felt stretched pretty thin. Especially since she was also supposed to attend the student council meeting to discuss plans for the meeting with the superintendent. Ms. Chu had a way of sending for her whenever Ernest really got out of control, and it was always at the most inconvenient times.

She could hear laughter even before she opened the door to his third-grade classroom—loud laughter. Ms. Chu was standing in front of the room, looking helpless and desperate. As for Ernest, he was sitting in his seat, and all the other kids were looking at him, laughing their heads off. All she could see when she first came into the classroom was the back of his head. He wasn't saying anything, but the kids around him were cracking up.

What was he doing?

"Oh, Genevieve . . ." Ms. Chu's voice was tragic. "He won't stop."

Gen walked around to face him, and there he sat, one finger up his nose.

"Ernest," she said severely, "did you hear what Dad said yesterday? Didn't you promise him . . ."

Ernest removed his finger from his nose. "I promised not to speak out, and I'm not. But I never promised Dad I wouldn't put my finger up my nose."

CHAPTER THREE

■ ■ ■ ■ ■

Many of Gen's friends were also in the cooking club. They exchanged recipes during club time and brought in special treats to exchange with the other members.

On the day Ms. Chu had called her down to Ernest's classroom, Gen had brought in her family's special chocolate-chip cake. She and Ernest both loved that cake more than any other, and Mom always made it for their birthdays. Now that Gen was eleven, she could bake it herself. Ernest liked to help and, if she was in a good mood, she let him. He loved the raw batter best of all and always pleaded with her to leave some in the bowl. She almost liked him when they baked that cake together. It was one of the few things they agreed on.

Like the glass slipper, the recipe for that cake came down from Grandmother Perl, Mom's mother. She was still alive, Gen knew that. She lived in Stockton, where Mom and Dad both grew up. Grandmother Perl had never seen either Ernest or Gen, and Mom hadn't spoken to her in over twenty-five years.

"Why, Mom?" Gen kept asking.

"You wouldn't understand." Mom's face grew tight and angry.

"Just try, Mom. Was she cruel to you? Did she abuse you?"

"Stop using that word. No, she didn't physically abuse me, but . . ." Mom shook her head. "One day, when you're older . . ."

"When, Mom? When I'm twelve?"

"No, I don't think so. And I don't want to talk about it. So stop asking me! I mean it!"

Mom's voice rose. She had the kind of voice that matched her moods. When she was cheerful, her voice rippled, sweet and low. When she began to get angry, her voice rose hard and sharp, and when she really lost her temper, it became shrill and piercing like a smoke alarm. Right now it was somewhere in the middle, so Gen dropped the subject.

Her father never exactly grew angry. He just didn't answer.

"Come on, Dad, you can tell me. I won't tell Mom."

"There's nothing to tell," Dad said, pulling up his newspaper so she couldn't see his face.

"Dad!" She peered at him over his newspaper. "Why is Mom so angry? And I guess you're angry, too, because you're not in touch with Grandmother Perl either. Was she mean to you? Did she try to stop the two of you from getting married? I know she wasn't at your wedding."

"It was a very small wedding," Dad mumbled.

"But your parents were both there, and your sister and brother, too. How come Mom's parents weren't there? Her father was still alive then. She was their only kid. I bet it had something to do with you, isn't that right, Dad?"

"You have to ask your mother, Gen."

"I have asked her, but she keeps saying I wouldn't understand, and that she'll tell me when I'm older."

"Well, I guess you'll have to wait till then," Dad said, shaking his head over the sports page and pretending to be engrossed in what he was reading. "They need a new pitcher," he said. "That's what the problem is."

In the wedding picture, Mom was wearing a pink, frilly dress with a white jacket and a white flower in her hair. Dad wore a suit with a green-striped tie. He still had that tie, even though it was nearly twenty-five years old. Both of them looked very happy, and Dad's family looked happy, too.

Dad's parents were both dead now, and his brother, Joe, was in the army, stationed in Germany. They hardly ever saw him and his family. But Dad's sister, Aunt Beth, lived in Novato with her husband, Josh, and their boys, Jason and Pete. Both families got together often, and Gen and her aunt were very close. Aunt Beth said that she had always wanted a daughter and still did, even though Uncle Josh said that another boy like his two boys would kill him. Gen thought her cousins were pests, like most boys, but not in the same league as Ernest. Jason was seven and Pete was five. They were always much worse when Ernest was around.

The families were celebrating Thanksgiving in Novato that year, and Gen was helping Aunt Beth stuff celery with cream cheese and olives. Mom and Dad were in the dining room with Uncle Josh, moving chairs around the table and getting it set.

"You knew my Grandmother Perl, didn't you, Aunt Beth?"

Aunt Beth smoothed cream cheese into a small piece of celery with a tiny crown of green leaves at the top. When she filled her celery stalks, she always seemed to know exactly how much cream cheese to add. Hers looked smooth and clean, with no extra blobs clinging to the leaves. Gen's celery stalks always rose bumpily in the middle and usually had flecks of cream cheese all over them.

"Gen, darling, please don't start that again. Would you hand me that bowl of radishes? Thanks."

Gen watched Aunt Beth begin to transform the radishes into roses with exquisite, intact petals.

"But why do you all make such a mystery of it? Something terrible must have happened. I just want you to tell me if she was a cruel, nasty woman who abused my mother."

Aunt Beth paused, a half-transformed radish in her hand. "You know, Gen, I'm six years younger than your parents, so I really didn't know your grandmother very well. I just saw her shopping sometimes. Your grandfather, too. He seemed like a nice, friendly man. He always had a smile on his face."

"So what happened?"

Aunt Beth resumed whittling her radish. "You'll find out one day, darling. It's not for me to tell you—you shouldn't even ask me. And besides, I really don't know the whole story."

Pete came howling into the kitchen. "Jason won't let me into his room," he cried. "He wants to play with Ernest all by himself."

"Tell him I said he has to play with you," Aunt Beth said mildly. "Tell him I said . . ."

But then there came a loud crash from upstairs, followed by Uncle Josh shouting.

"They've probably been jumping on Jason's bed again," Aunt Beth said tranquilly, arranging all of the radishes around a mound of hummus. "That bed always breaks whenever he and Ernest jump on it."

Mom and Dad had five photo albums of their family. There were two of Mom and Dad as kids, and the other three were of Gen and Ernest with or without their parents. In Mom's album, there were a number of her as a child with her parents, so Gen knew what they looked like. Her Grandfather Perl was a tall man and her Grandmother Perl looked a lot like Mom. The picture Gen liked the most was one at a picnic. Mom must have been about her own age and was carrying a watermelon basket filled with chunks of fruit. Mom was smiling. Right behind her, also smiling, was Grandmother Perl carrying a cake. Gen always felt hungry when she looked at that picture, because she knew what kind of cake Grandmother Perl was carrying.

CHAPTER FOUR

▪▪▪▪▪

The idea for a surprise twenty-fifth wedding anniversary party came to Gen one day in January when Ernest brought a note home from the principal. It said:

Dear Mr. & Mrs. Bishop,

Ernest continues to run out of the school yard during recess. I am asking him to write 100 times "I will not run out of the school yard during recess," and to turn it in to me personally tomorrow morning. I would appreciate your complete cooperation in this matter. Please call me regarding our telephone conference the other day.

Sincerely,
Lucy Carrera

"Go!" Dad thundered at Ernest in his nearly scary voice. "Go to your room this minute and start writing."

"Okay, Dad." Ernest grinned and scampered up the stairs.

Gen was watching TV in the living room, and her parents, in the adjoining kitchen, lowered their voices. As soon as Gen heard the lowered voices, she automatically moved closer to the wall between the living room and the kitchen.

"I don't know," Mom was saying. "Maybe we should."

"No!" Dad said. "I don't want them to mess around with him. He's just curious, and maybe a little restless. He'll grow out of it."

They were only worrying about Ernest again. Gen had heard this type of conversation so many times, it was boring. She nearly returned to the TV, but then Mom said, "I agreed to call her tomorrow. I'll do it from the store. I don't want either Gen or Ernest to hear."

Gen remained where she was.

"Every year there's some kind of fancy name for curious, restless boys," Dad grumbled.

"Attention Deficit Disorder," Mom said. "That's what Ms. Carrera thinks it might be. She says a number of kids at school have been tested and diagnosed, and that the drug can really help these kids focus. I don't know, Dan; maybe we ought to have him tested."

"Remember what I was like at his age?" Dad said.

"Oh boy, do I ever!" Mom was laughing now. "I think you were even worse than he is."

"I wouldn't go that far." Now Dad was laughing, too. "My poor mother—she spent half her life at school. But in those days, they just called you a rotten kid."

"That time," Mom said, "you got up and started dancing on the tables when the music teacher was trying to have us sing 'Jingle Bells.' When was that—fifth grade?"

"Oh, come on, give me a break. It must have been in second grade."

"No, it was fifth or maybe even sixth. Because I remember the music teacher—Mr. Hermanson. He was a little guy, and his face grew so red. I remember thinking he looked like a strawberry."

"Well, I guess I was just getting into the Christmas spirit. Anyway, what I'm trying to say is some boys are like that. My dad was no doll either, and he had a hard time trying to read me the riot act. But—hey—I outgrew it, right?"

"Oh, sure, Dan, when you were about thirty-five, you outgrew it."

Here Gen heard a little scuffle and some squishy laughing. "Shh! Shh!" Mom said, sounding out of breath. Gen leaned hard against the wall.

"Well, at least we have Gen," Dad said.

"Yes," Mom agreed. "She really is a darling."

Gen grinned. She mentally patted herself on the head.

"Not a minute's worry with her," Dad said. "She's a lot like you. You were the same way when you were her age—the nicest, smartest, prettiest kid in the whole school. I always loved you, Amy, starting in second grade, but I never thought you liked me."

"I didn't in second grade," Mom said, "but later, in ninth grade or maybe tenth grade."

"Such a long time ago," Dad said. "Most of our lives. We've been married—what is it now?"

"It will be twenty-five years in June."

"But we knew each other for years before that."

"Twenty-five years," Mom repeated. "Twenty-five years!"

That's when Gen decided to give them a surprise twenty-fifth anniversary party. Even though Mom and Dad eventually resumed their conversation about whether or not Ernest should be tested for Attention Deficit Disorder, Gen removed herself from the wall, turned off the TV, tiptoed to the phone in the hall, and called Aunt Beth.

"I want to give Mom and Dad a surprise party for their twenty-fifth anniversary. Will you help me?"

"Twenty-five years!" Aunt Beth said. "I can't believe it."

"What do you think? We could have a party with all their friends and the family and . . ."

"Potluck!" Aunt Beth said firmly. "That's the best way to do it. Everybody can bring something, and we'll order a cake and have champagne for the grown-ups and sparkling cider for the kids."

"And you can do all those fancy things you do with the veggies, and I'll get my cooking club to help out."

"And we can send out invitations showing their wedding picture." Aunt Beth sounded just as excited as Gen.

"Gen! Ernest!" Mom called out from the kitchen. "Dinner's ready."

"I've got to go now, Aunt Beth."

"I'm not finished," Ernest yelled down from upstairs.

"You'll finish after dinner," Dad told him. "Just get yourself down here right now."

"It's a wonderful idea, Gen," Aunt Beth enthused. "You really are a darling."

Lots of people said she was a darling, Gen thought, as she hung up the phone. She knew she was like Mom. She knew they looked alike, and Mom kept saying how much they resembled each other in so many different ways. She paused a little while, thinking proudly about the differences between Ernest and herself. He was a problem child, causing their parents many hours of worry, while she, as Dad said, never gave them a minute's concern. Suddenly, amazingly, she was crying. Why? She wondered why. It was hard, she suddenly realized, very hard. Always being good. Always being a darling.

Just this day at school, she had overheard Karen Knipper telling Jill Ewing that she, Gen, was a show-off.

"No, she's not," Jill said.

Gen was working on the computer, putting together some ideas for her speech to the superintendent on why class size should be reduced, and she pretended to keep on working.

"Yes, she is. And she's a real goody-goody—Miss Perfect. Never does anything wrong. Always making nicey-nice to all the teachers. She doesn't have an original idea in her head."

"Shh!" Jill cautioned. "She's right over there. She'll hear you."

"Who cares!" Karen said, but she lowered her voice, and the two of them moved out of hearing.

Lots of people told Gen that Karen was jealous. After all, this was the second time she had run against Gen for class president and lost. Last time a few kids had voted for Karen, but this time Gen had been elected almost unanimously. Only one vote for Karen, and it was obvious where that one came from. Gen felt embarrassed for Karen and went out of her way to smile and speak pleasantly to her. But Karen kept giving her cold, angry looks and saying mean things about her, not even behind her back. Why should Karen hate her so much? Gen could not think of anybody else who hated her, and it was upsetting. Maybe she was doing something wrong. But what was it?

Back in second grade, when neither of them ran for anything, they had almost been friends. They even had a play date one day over at Karen's house. Gen remembered a beautiful garden, and she also remembered bringing a bunch of pink flowers home.

But already in second grade, Gen had more friends than she knew what to do with. She guessed she was the most popular kid in her class. She had always been the most popular kid in her class. Even the boys liked her, and even more amazingly, everybody voted for her as president, both in fifth grade and now in sixth.

She tried to get along with everyone, and certainly she had never done anything nasty to Karen and never said mean things about her.

But today at school, after Karen and Jill moved away, she felt tears in her eyes and had to bend down under the table, pretending to look for something on the floor.

And now again she was crying. Why? Mom and

Dad hadn't said anything mean like Karen had. Why should she be crying when both Dad and Mom thought she was so wonderful?

And why did Karen hate her so much?

Why?

CHAPTER FIVE

Ernest brought another note home the next day from the principal. It said:

> *Dear Mr. & Mrs. Bishop,*
>
> *Ernest did write 100 times "I will not run out of the school yard during recess," but he wrote each sentence in a different color marker or colored pencil. He appeared to have enjoyed himself, although the assignment was meant as a punishment. I have asked him to redo the assignment in only one color, using a regular pencil. Please supervise his work and make sure he understands that this is a punishment.*
>
> *Sincerely,*
> *Lucy Carrera*

Gen shared her plans for the surprise twenty-fifth anniversary party with her cooking club on Tuesday morning, which was club day. The members all agreed to help and also promised not to tell anybody else.

That same evening Mrs. Ewing, Jill's mother, called.

"She wants to talk to *you*," Mom said, shrugging and handing her the phone. "She says it's something about the homework."

"Gen," whispered Mrs. Ewing, "I'm so excited about your idea for the surprise party for your parents' anniversary."

"Umm," Gen answered, watching Dad as he carried some laundry up the stairs.

"I understand," Mrs. Ewing said. "You can't talk because they're around. But I wanted you to know that I really want to help, and so does my husband. Just give me a ring when the coast is clear."

Once Dad was safely up the stairs, Gen whispered, "But it's supposed to be a secret."

"Oh, I know. I know," Mrs. Ewing whispered back, "and you don't have to worry about Jim and me. We won't tell a soul."

The next day, Wednesday, Andrea Page's dad honked at her as she was on her way home from school. He pulled his car over to the curb. Inside, Gen saw Andrea and her twin sisters, Jeannie and Joanie. "Hi, Gen," Mr. Page said.

"I just wanted you to know that Gail and I are ready for our assignments."

"Assignments?" Gen asked. Andrea waved at her.

"For the surprise party. Listen, sweetie, if you decide to send out invitations, just let me handle it for you."

"But it's supposed to be a secret."

"Don't worry about that. We won't tell a soul."

Wednesday afternoon, Ernest's note from the principal said:

> Dear Mr. & Mrs. Bishop,
>   Although Ernest wrote "I will not run out of the yard" one hundred times in regular pencil as I instructed, he managed to dot the i in "will" one hundred different ways. He refuses to understand that a punishment is not meant to be fun. I have decided not to ask him to repeat the assignment, but to stay for an hour after school in my office tomorrow.
>   Sincerely,
>   Lucy Carrera

"Gen," Ernest said, catching up with her as she and a couple of her friends were walking home from school on Friday, "can I see you—alone?"

"You can see me alone when we get home from school," Gen told him.

"But usually Mom comes home early from the store," he said. "Please! It's important."

Gen noticed that he looked unhappy. It was very seldom that Ernest looked unhappy. Generally, his teachers or parents or sister were the ones who looked unhappy.

"Well, what is it?" she asked, falling back with him.

Ernest began crying.

Gen felt her fists clench. Not that she planned to use them on Ernest. Gen hardly ever actually hit Ernest, or anybody else, for that matter. But, irritated as she was most of the time with her brother, she could not bear it if anybody else made him unhappy.

"What is it?" she demanded. "Did somebody bother you? Who was it?"

"You!" Ernest blubbered. "It was you."

"Me?"

"Everybody." Ernest wept, big tears flowing down his cheeks. He looked like a normal little eight-year-old when he cried—which was seldom. "Everybody knows about the surprise anniversary party except me. Everybody is helping out except me. How come, Gen? How come you didn't tell me?"

Gen unclenched her fists. "Oh, Ernest," she told him, "it was supposed to be a secret—between me, Aunt Beth, and my cooking club."

"Well, Joey Uchida told me about it. He said his mother is going to make a salad."

"Joey Uchida? I don't even know who he is. He doesn't have a sister in my club."

"No, but his cousin, Ruth Shori, is in your club. Everybody knows but me. How come you didn't tell me?"

"I would have told you, Ernest, but I wanted it to be a secret."

"I'm their kid, too," Ernest howled. "I want to do something for the surprise party. And if you won't let me, I'll make my own surprise party for them."

Gen laughed. First, Ernest looked up angrily at her; then he began smiling. "So, can I help too, Gen?" he said finally, putting a hand on her arm. She didn't shake it off.

"Sure, Ernest," she said. "Why not? Everybody else is."

On the Monday before the Tuesday that Gen was going with the delegation to the superintendent's office, Warren Heller, the class's vice president, was out sick. He was planning to go along with Gen the next day. He and Gen had worked together on their speeches urging the superintendent to reduce class size from thirty-plus students in the fifth and sixth grades to no more than twenty.

Mr. Robbins called Gen up to his desk.

"We'd better pick an alternate," he said. "Warren's

mother just called and said he had a bad ear infection and a high fever. Who do you think would be a good person to go in his place?"

To her amazement, Gen said, without hesitating, "Karen Knipper."

She watched Mr. Robbins's face tighten in surprise. She guessed he was going to object, and she was already considering recommending Bob Gee. But then Mr. Robbins nodded. "Good idea!" he said. "It's time she got a little recognition. Karen, would you come up here, please."

Karen moved slowly toward Mr. Robbins's desk. Her face, as ever, was surly, and she narrowed her eyes and turned a tight, suspicious look at Gen.

"Karen," Mr. Robbins asked, "how would you like to go as a delegate to the superintendent's office tomorrow in place of Warren? He's sick, and Gen thought you might be a good alternate."

Karen hesitated and looked back and forth at Gen and Mr. Robbins. Gen smiled at her and tried to look encouraging.

"What would I have to do?" she finally asked Mr. Robbins.

"Well, most of the other kids in the delegation have written short speeches trying to convince the superintendent of the importance of smaller class size . . ."

Then Gen burst in, trying to be helpful. "Maybe we

could get Warren's speech and you could just read his, since you don't have much time to prepare your own."

Karen stiffened, and glared at Gen. "I don't need Warren's speech, thank you very much. I'm perfectly capable of writing my own."

CHAPTER SIX

▪▪▪▪▪

"You what?" Mom asked.

Ernest repeated what he had just said. "I want to make a valentine for everybody in my class."

Mom shook her head doubtfully.

"Nobody makes valentines for everybody when they're in third grade," Gen said. "Only kindergarten kids make them for everybody, and most of the time they buy them in the store."

"Well, I want to," Ernest insisted.

"Why?" Gen demanded. "You never gave anybody in your class a valentine before. Not even in kindergarten."

"I just want to. Mom, why can't I? I'm going to make them myself. I'm going to cut pictures out of catalogs, and I'll just need a few dollars for some fancy paper to paste things on. I'm going to fold them over so I won't need envelopes. Come on, Mom."

"I don't know, Ernest."

"Please!"

Mom turned to Gen. "Well, it really doesn't sound as if anything bad can happen, does it?"

"I'm not sure," Gen said vaguely.

She had other things to worry about. One other thing especially—Karen. Although their meeting with the superintendent had gone very well, Karen seemed to hate her just as much as before, or maybe even more. Karen's speech was pretty good. In fact, Gen had to admit that Karen's speech was not only good, it was surprisingly funny. The superintendent had laughed out loud when Karen accused him of being responsible for the recent epidemic of lice because thirty students and their teacher in a small classroom would have their heads much closer together than they would if there were only twenty.

After the meeting, Gen had even detached herself from the excited, laughing group of delegates to find Karen. There she was, as usual, standing by herself and looking bored.

"That was a very funny speech," Gen said to her.

"Thank you," Karen replied, almost rudely, turning

away and pretending to look for somebody who wasn't there.

"Karen," Gen said, "why . . . ?"

"Why what?" Karen asked sullenly.

Gen could feel the tears rising again, and she said quickly, "Why . . . why . . . do you hate me so much?"

"I don't hate you at all," Karen said hatefully. "I don't even think about you—ever."

"Well," Gen said, "if you don't ever think about me, why are you always saying mean things about me? I never did anything to you." She had to gulp hard to force the tears back.

"You give yourself a lot of credit," Karen said furiously. "You think you're more important than anybody else."

"No, I don't," Gen said.

"Just because they all vote for you—it's only because you're always saying nice things to everybody. You never have any opinions of your own. All you care about is making everybody like you. Well, I don't like you. So, just bug off and leave me alone."

Now, Karen began to choke up. Gen saw that she was crying, and she began crying, too. But Karen ran off and didn't notice.

In school her cooking club made heart-shaped cookies for everybody in the class. She and her friends exchanged valentines, and a few mysterious ones were dropped on her desk that made her ears tingle. They might have come from boys.

The day after Valentine's Day, Ernest brought home another note from the principal.

> Dear Mr. & Mrs. Bishop,
>   Ernest gave a Valentine's card to every child in the class and to Ms. Chu as well. Her card seemed appropriate, but each of the other cards contained an insult if you take the first letter of each word in the sentence. Considering that there are twenty-nine students in Ernest's class, he apparently knows a great number of unpleasant words. I enclose several cards he made so you can see for yourselves.
>   Please give this matter your serious attention.
>   Lucy Carrera

One of the valentines, addressed to Joan Pepper, contained this message: SKIP LIGHTLY OVER BLOOD. Followed by: HAPPY VALENTINE'S DAY from ERNEST BISHOP.

Another one, addressed to Fred Wong, said: NEVER EVER REPEAT DIRT. It was also followed by: HAPPY VALENTINE'S DAY from ERNEST BISHOP.

The third one, Mom didn't even show to Gen. She

pulled Ernest into her bedroom, closed the door, and yelled so loud that Gen, standing outside in the hall, had no trouble hearing.

"How could you do such a disgusting thing?" she said. "To send Valentine's cards to people and insult them? And some of those words—I don't even know where you picked them up."

Ernest shouted back. He sounded angry. "Ms. Chu wants us to learn new words. She keeps saying she's going to give A's to the kids who come up with the most new words and show how to use them in a sentence. I used a new word in every valentine, and I know I spelled them right. She didn't say they had to be nice words. It's not fair!"

At dinner even Dad seemed to take Ernest's side. "It's not like it was a regular assignment," he said.

"And I worked hard," Ernest insisted. "I even looked some of them up in the dictionary."

"And actually," Dad continued, holding the valentine to Joan Pepper, "you can't say it's not original."

"But it's disgusting," Gen said. "He knows very well he's not supposed to use words like that in school."

"Ms. Chu even promised to give extra credit if you came up with more than ten new words. I came up with twenty-eight—twenty-nine, really, but Eddie Snow was absent."

"And look how well he spells," Dad beamed. "I was

never such a good speller. I didn't know how to spell *vampire* until I was nine or ten at least."

Gen was curious. "Who did you give the vampire card to?"

"Carrie Fine." Ernest laughed. "That was my best sentence, too. I said: V̲ACCINATIONS A̲RE M̲EAN P̲ARTICULARLY I̲F R̲ABBITS E̲AT."

"You wrote that?" Even Gen was impressed. "But you were never good in spelling. When did you learn?"

Ernest shrugged. "I guess for Valentine's Day. But I think Ms. Chu is a l-i-a-r, and Ms. Carrera is an a—"

"That's enough of that!" Mom said, trying to look serious.

Gen noticed that Dad and Mom never exchanged Valentine's cards and never gave each other gifts.

"How come?" she wanted to know.

"Oh, Gen," Mom said, "maybe we did when we were kids. But now we both think it's just a holiday that's promoted by the greeting-card companies."

"But isn't it nice when you're in love to send somebody a card or give him or her a present?"

"Well, sure," Dad said, "but it doesn't have to be on Valentine's Day. It can be any day that's special."

"Like what?" Gen said.

"Oh, I guess like birthdays. After all, Valentine's Day isn't really a special day for one special person, like a birthday. If you love somebody, you're glad that person was born, so you feel like celebrating that day."

"Any other day?" Ernest asked casually.

"Well, okay, Christmas." Mom picked it up. "I think it's gotten away from what it really is about, but, okay, when you have kids especially, Christmas is really fun. And Thanksgiving—even if everybody celebrates it differently. We each have our own special things to be thankful about."

"Uh-huh," Ernest nodded. "Anything else?"

Dad laughed. "What is this—the Inquisition? Well, I suppose the Fourth of July is fun. Remember, Amy, how we used to watch the fireworks? All the kids from school used to go up to Junipero Hill, and some of us used to set cherry bombs under cans, and . . ."

"And, Dan, do you remember when you nearly blew off Debbie Mendoza's finger, and . . ."

Gen grabbed Ernest and yanked him off to her room while her parents reminisced.

"You're going to have to stop asking questions like that," she told him. "You'll make them suspicious."

"No, I won't," he said. "They never figure anything out before it happens."

"Isn't it funny," Gen said, "that they don't celebrate Valentine's Day or anniversaries?"

"Valentine's Day is a dumb holiday," Ernest said, "but maybe I'll make them a card for their anniversary."

"Like the cards you made for the kids in your class?"

Ernest grinned. "You should have seen Carrie Fine's face when she figured out her card. She's the one who finked and told Ms. Chu."

"Anyway," Gen said, "I wonder if it has something to do with Grandmother Perl."

"Who?"

"You know—Grandmother Perl, Mom's mother. I told you about her. We've never met her, and she and Mom haven't talked to each other in twenty-five years."

"Is she still alive?"

"You know she is. She lives in Stockton."

"Well, why don't you just call her up and ask her?"

"Oh, no! I couldn't do that."

"Well, I could," said Ernest.

CHAPTER SEVEN

Gen began discussing the menu for the twenty-fifth anniversary party with her cooking club.

"My Aunt Beth thinks it should be potluck," she told them. "Each of us can make a dish, and maybe you can give your parents assignments...."

Jill interrupted. "Actually, my mom wants to make her garlic-cheese focaccia, and I know Ruth's mom has a fabulous eggplant-shrimp salad that she's making, and Mrs. Paxton wants to bring portobello mushrooms over polenta."

"Who's Mrs. Paxton?" Gen asked.

"Oh, she's my mom's friend—and she's president of the P.T.A. Your mom knows her. She's always buying things at the store."

"It shouldn't get too big," Gen insisted. "I was thinking maybe we'd have twenty-five to thirty people. Our house is pretty small for a huge party."

"The more people you have," Ruth said, "the more dishes they'll bring. Potlucks are more fun when there are lots of dishes to choose from."

"But I decided," Gen said, "to invite mostly friends and family—friends of my parents, I mean."

"Well, you can always open the garage door and fix up the garage. You know, hang up streamers and string some lights. My Uncle Joe is an electrician. I'll ask him to help out," said Sandra Ramos.

Mr. Robbins, their teacher, said he knew how to make the best pesto sauce in California. He promised to bring enough to cover ten pounds of pasta, preferably linguine, and he asked if he could bring a friend.

"It's getting out of hand," Gen complained to Aunt Beth over the phone. "Lots of people are planning to come even if I didn't actually invite them. What should I do?"

Aunt Beth laughed. "I just hope it will be a surprise. Your mother was saying the other day that she couldn't believe how you and Ernest were spending so much time together and not fighting as much as usual."

"I'm making him save his allowance," Gen said. "He's been giving me most of it every week, and I've been saving most of mine. And we each have money in the bank, if we need it, but Mom would be suspicious if we started withdrawing it."

"You won't need that much," Aunt Beth said. "People are bringing the food. Your uncle and I will supply the drinks. Wasn't there a father who offered to do the invitations?"

"Well, yes. But what about the decorations?"

"Okay—you and Ernest can pay for those. But that shouldn't cost a lot. There's that party outlet store in the Mission District. I'll drive you over there when we get closer to the day."

"And what about a fancy cake that says 'Happy Anniversary'?"

"Oh, I can order one from the Potters."

"Who?"

"Alison and Pete Potter. He's a baker. Your father went to school with Pete's brother, Nick. He lives up the block from us."

"Who? Nick?"

"No. Nick's in Washington D.C. His brother Pete and his wife Alison."

"Oh!"

"It's getting way too big," Gen moaned to Ernest. "I don't even know who's coming anymore. I don't know where we can put them all."

"I have her telephone number," Ernest said.

"Whose telephone number?"

"Grandmother Perl. Her name is Adrienne Perl, and she lives on San Marcos Street in Stockton."

"How did you find that out?"

"I called Information. They told me."

Gen looked at her brother nervously. It bothered her that he had come up with Grandmother Perl's number. She didn't know why it bothered her, but it did. Too many things were bothering her these days.

"I think we should call her up," Ernest said.

"But why?"

"I think we should call her up and invite her to the party."

"Look, Ernest," Gen told him, "we don't know why Mom is so angry at her. Maybe she's a terrible person. Maybe she was mean to Mom and Dad."

"It's supposed to be a surprise party," Ernest insisted, "so let's invite her. Then it will be a double surprise party."

Something stirred inside Gen. Even though it still bothered her that Ernest was the one who went ahead and found Grandmother Perl's number, something said, *Now! Do it now!* Mom and Dad were both working late, doing inventory at the store. Nobody was home who could come barging in and demand who they were calling. "Maybe she's not home," Gen said weakly.

Ernest held out a piece of paper. "Here's the number," he said. "You do it."

The stirring became a drumming in her head. *Do it! Do it! Don't wait! Don't wait!* it pounded. Underneath it all, Gen knew that this was not right. It was not right to do something her parents would not approve of. It was bad. It was very bad.

She grabbed the paper, rushed out into the hall, and dialed the number. She stood, frozen, holding the phone tightly in her hand. Ernest stood there next to her, looking up into her face.

It rang once.

It rang twice.

"Hello," said a woman's voice.

"Uh—hello," answered Gen.

"Who is this?" the woman demanded. She had a quick, sharp voice.

"Uh—is this—uh—Mrs. Perl?"

"I'm not interested," the woman said, and hung up.

"She hung up," Gen said, putting down the receiver. She felt relieved. She had nearly done something her parents would not approve of. It was wrong. She never should have listened to Ernest.

"Here, give me the phone," Ernest said. He looked down at the paper and dialed the number.

"Hello," he said finally. "Is this Mrs. Perl? . . . Wait a minute! Don't hang up. This is Ernest Bishop. I'm . . . I think . . . I'm your grandson. What?"

Gen watched his face wrinkling up. She was listening very hard. She could hear sounds on the other end of the receiver, but it wasn't clear what Grandmother Perl was saying.

Then Ernest shook his head. His face was puzzled. He held out the phone to her. "Here," he whispered. "You'd better talk to her."

"Why?" Gen whispered back.

"Because . . . I think . . . she's crying."

CHAPTER EIGHT

■ ■ ■ ■ ■

"Don't tell anybody!" Gen warned Ernest after she hung up. "You've got a big mouth."

"Not as big as yours," he snapped. "Because of you, everybody knows about the party. I didn't tell anyone. They told me. Anyway, what did she say?"

"Not much—she just kept crying and crying. I think she was really glad to hear from us."

"So why was she crying?"

"I don't know why."

"How come you didn't invite her to the party? Maybe that would have cheered her up."

"I didn't have a chance. I hardly said anything to her. She just wanted to know if Mom was all right. Maybe she thought something had happened to her. And then she said . . . did Mom want to talk to her. When I said no, Mom didn't even know we were calling, she started crying again. So—you heard—I said maybe we should call her again tomorrow. And she said, yes, that would be a good idea."

"Are you going to ask her tomorrow why she and Mom are so mad at each other?"

"I guess so—I mean—if she stops crying."

"I don't know," Mom said that evening over dinner. "Business is really picking up all of a sudden."

"Well, it's spring," Dad said. "People start fixing up their houses and buying new curtains. I had a bunch today buying curtain rods."

"Well, maybe so," Mom said doubtfully. "But some of them I never saw before, and they all seemed to think they knew us. One of them said her sister's daughter was in Ernest's class."

Dad laughed. "Ernest is pretty famous, I guess."

"What's her name?" Ernest asked.

"Oh, I don't know," Mom said, "but she was very friendly and talked about passing through Stockton once. Now how did she happen to bring up Stockton? Almost as if she knew I came from Stockton."

"Mom," Gen said, anxious to change the subject, "do you have any extra baskets you could let me have for

Easter? I'm arranging an Easter egg hunt for the kinder-gartners."

"I'll look around the store," Mom said, "but lately I don't seem to have a quiet moment."

They weren't able to call Grandmother Perl the next day because Ernest was suspended from school. The letter from the principal said:

> *Dear Mr. & Mrs. Bishop,*
>
> *As I explained to you over the phone, Ernest is in serious trouble. He was seen stealing money out of Ms. Chu's desk during recess. When he was accused and confronted by two witnesses, he threw a book at Ms. Chu and tried to attack his accusers.*
>
> *I would like to see you both in my office tomor-row morning at 9 A.M., with Ernest. I realize you have a store, so I would be willing to meet with just one of you. Ernest will be suspended from school for the rest of the week, and I must tell you that I am con-sidering having him transferred to another school.*
>
> *Lucy Carrera*

Both Mom and Dad were waiting for Ernest when he arrived home. They had left Roger Yamato, their part-time high-school worker, alone in the store. For the first time Gen could remember, Dad was not understanding.

And, for the first time, his voice was not pretend-serious. It sounded like a foghorn. He grabbed Ernest as soon as he stepped through the door, shook him furiously, and slapped him across the face.

"Never!" Dad roared, shaking him some more. "Never! Never again! Do you hear me?"

"Calm down, Dan," Mom said, putting a hand on Dad's arm. "Better let me handle it."

"You stay out of it, Amy," he yelled, shaking off her arm. Gen had never seen him so angry in her whole life. "You should know how serious this is."

"Let me go!" Ernest cried, struggling. "I didn't do it."

Dad put his face very close to Ernest's. "This is no joke, buddy," he yelled. "This is the kind of thing that leads to real trouble. It's criminal to steal money. Criminals end up in jail. Do you understand?"

He resumed shaking Ernest so hard that Mom screamed, "Stop it, Dan. You'll hurt him."

"I want to hurt him," Dad yelled. "I don't want him ever to forget this."

Mom grabbed Ernest away from Dad and shouted, "You're going crazy, Dan. Control yourself!"

Ernest's face was white except for the red slap mark across one cheek. "I didn't do it!" he yelled. "I didn't do it!"

"Don't lie to me," Dad yelled back. "Two kids saw you do it, and you threw a book at your teacher."

"I didn't do it!" Ernest repeated. He pulled away from Mom and ran up the stairs. Gen could hear the door of his room slam.

Dad started up the stairs after him, but Mom actually got in front of him and said, "I'm not going to let you go near him until you calm down."

"Amy," Dad thundered, "he has to understand how serious this is. You know what this can lead to."

"He's eight years old, Dan. Aren't you forgetting that?"

"And aren't you forgetting . . ."

Gen left them there, arguing on the stairs. Her own fists were clenched, and the familiar anger she felt when somebody else made Ernest cry began rising inside her. Sure, she usually enjoyed it when Mom screamed at Ernest, and she always enjoyed it when her parents took her side against his. But this time it was different. Was she the only one who really heard Ernest say he didn't do it?

She hurried up the stairs and tapped at his door. No answer. She pushed open the door and came inside. Ernest was banging his fists on a wall and did not hear her.

"Ernest," she said. "Ernest."

He turned and shook his head. He wasn't crying, and Dad's slap mark had nearly faded. He looked furious.

"Nobody believes me," he yelled. "I didn't do it."

"But those two kids saw you."

"They took the money. I saw them. Then when they heard Ms. Chu coming, they dropped it in front of me and said I did it. And she didn't even listen to me."

"Who were those kids?"

"Carrie Fine and Lisa Jordan. Just because they're girls—and smart—and goody-goodies, she believed them. But I didn't do it, Gen, I didn't do it. And Dad didn't even listen."

Suddenly Ernest's shoulders began heaving, and then all of him was shaking, and he started crying in a terrible, scary way.

Gen grabbed him and dragged him down the stairs to where both of her parents stood, still arguing.

"Listen," she shouted. "Ernest didn't do it. What kind of parents are you that you don't even believe your own kid?"

She pulled Ernest over to her. He had stopped crying and trembling and was looking up at her in amazement.

"How come you're so ready to believe the worst, and not give him a chance to explain? It was those other two kids—those girls—who stole the money. Ernest saw them, and everybody believed them. Even the two of you."

Mom stood motionless, her mouth open.

"And you," Gen said to her father, "you hit him, and you didn't let him explain. What kind of a father are you that you didn't even listen to your own kid? Ernest may get into trouble sometimes, but he's never stolen anything before, and he's also never lied."

Dad took a deep breath, and then he said in a very low voice, "Ernest—I want to know the truth—Ernest?"

"I told you the truth," Ernest said, straightening up. Now the color had returned to his face, and Gen noticed even his ears had turned red. "Carrie and Lisa took the money and dropped it in front of me when Ms. Chu came in the room. She wouldn't listen to me. That's why I threw the book at her. I wish it was a rock."

"Oh, Ernest," Mom said, reaching out for him. "My poor boy!"

"I . . . I'm sorry, Ernest," Dad said, also reaching out for him. "I'll make it up to you. And tomorrow, Mom and I will both go to school and talk to that principal and to your teacher."

"I'm going to go, too," Gen said. "I'm going to tell her what I think."

"I bet she won't believe you," Ernest said.

"Who cares if she doesn't!" Gen said. "We'll go to the superintendent if she doesn't. We'll go to the mayor. . . ."

She kept on talking, but all the time she felt more

and more helpless and frightened. Everything seemed suddenly out of control. Dad's fury! She'd never seen Dad like that, and she felt almost guilty because she'd always wanted him to get really angry at Ernest. But not like that!

CHAPTER NINE

■■■■■

Ms. Carrera ended up believing Ernest. And so did Ms. Chu. Both apologized many, many times, especially after Carrie and Lisa confessed. The letter that came home that afternoon with Ernest said:

> Dear Mr. & Mrs. Bishop and Genevieve,
>   Thank you for being so understanding. Both Ms. Chu and I regret very much how badly we handled this whole incident, and want to apologize again to your whole family for all the trauma I'm sure it created.
>   Carrie and Lisa have been suspended for the rest of the week and have promised to write letters of apology to Ernest. Of course, as I have pointed out to

Ernest, even though he was completely innocent in this particular case, he has been in trouble so many times in the past that it seemed as if his word was not as believable as Carrie's and Lisa's. I hope this will be a useful lesson to him and, I suppose, to us as well. You certainly cannot always tell a book by its cover.

> *Sincerely,*
> *Lucy Carrera*

For the rest of the week, Mom and Dad couldn't do enough for Ernest. Dad took him to the toy store and let him buy the ugliest set of Power Rangers Gen had ever seen. Mom spoke to him in her softest, sweetest voice, even when he managed to tear his new jacket climbing over the school fence. For a few days, even Gen regarded him almost with affection.

It was during this time that Ernest reminded her they had forgotten all about Grandmother Perl.

"We were supposed to call her back three days ago," he said.

"Oh, right," Gen said. "I forgot all about her, and now Mom's been staying home in the afternoons so she can be nice to you."

"We'll have to go outside," Ernest said. "How much is a call to Stockton anyway?"

They took a bunch of dimes and quarters and called Grandmother Perl from a phone booth near school.

The phone rang only once before she answered it. "Hello!"

"Uh—hello—uh—Mrs. Perl? This is Gen Bishop."

"I thought you had decided not to call me," she said. "I thought maybe your mother found out and made you stop."

"Oh, no, nothing like that. It's just Ernest . . ."

"Don't tell her," Ernest whispered loudly. "I don't want you to tell her."

"What doesn't he want you to tell me? Is it your mother? Is she all right?"

"She's fine. Really, Mrs. Perl, she's fine. It's something to do with school—nothing important, really—and everything's fine now."

"Well, then . . ."

"Well . . ."

"Tell her about the party," Ernest said.

"What's that he's saying? What does he want you to tell me?"

That's when the operator interrupted and asked for more money.

Ernest insisted on putting the money in, only he didn't understand they just had to put in another fifty cents.

"You put too much money in," Gen told him. "It was only fifty cents, and you put in four quarters."

"Well, that's what you said—four quarters."

"Ernest, I said two."

"No, you didn't."

"Are you calling from a pay phone?" Grandmother Perl managed to say.

Ernest stepped on one of Gen's feet, and she poked him with her elbow. "Stop it," she told him. "Uh, yes, Mrs. Perl, because our mother is home today."

"Well, why don't you give me the number, and I'll call you right back."

Gen gave her the number and hung up. "She's calling us right back," she told Ernest, "and it's just as well, because you put in all those quarters. We would have run out."

"Well, you told me . . ."

"If you kids are finished with the phone," a man said, who had just hurried over, "I need to make a call."

"Well, we're not finished," Ernest said. "Somebody's calling us back, so you'll have to go find another phone."

"Look, this is important," said the man, "and you're not supposed to tie up a public phone."

"Says who?"

The phone rang. Gen picked it up. "Hello?" she said.

"Uh—hello—this is . . . this is . . ."

"I know," Gen said. "This is Mrs. Perl."

"Well, yes. What's going on there?"

"Oh, there's a man who wants to use the phone, and my brother is telling him he has to go find another one."

"How old is your brother?"

"He's eight."

"And you—how old are you?"

"I'm eleven."

"And what did you say your name was?"

"It's Genevieve, but everybody calls me Gen."

"It's hard to hear you. There's so much noise."

Ernest shouted something nasty at the man, who lunged toward him.

"What's going on there?" Mrs. Perl cried. "Is somebody hurting your brother?"

"Not really," Gen said, watching Ernest leap down the street, turning from time to time to make Power Ranger faces at the man, who was in clumsy pursuit.

"Well, there are so many weirdos around nowadays," Mrs. Perl said in a worried way. She sounded like an old lady. She sounded like a grandmother was supposed to sound. "Are you sure your brother is all right?"

Gen peered around the booth and saw the man leaning, breathless, against a light post. Ernest was dancing around and yelling something at him from further down the street. "You don't have to worry about my brother," she said. "He can take care of himself."

"What does he look like? I mean, your brother."

"Well, he's got curly blond hair and blue eyes, like Dad. Most people think he looks like Dad. But he has a mean smile. Dad doesn't have a mean smile."

"And—and you?"

"Well, I'm dark, and I have brown eyes. I guess I look like Mom."

Mrs. Perl just breathed loud.

"And maybe like you. My mom looks like you, doesn't she?"

"She did." Mrs. Perl sounded as if she were crying again. That's when Ernest came bounding back, huffing and puffing, but grinning. "Can I talk to her now?" he said breathlessly.

"My brother wants to talk to you," Gen said, handing Ernest the phone.

"Hello, Mrs. Perl. This is Ernest. What? What?" He shook his head and looked at Gen. "She's crying again. I always make her cry, even though I'm not doing anything. Ah, now she's talking. Yes. Yes. No, he didn't hurt me."

A woman came up to the telephone booth and looked at her watch.

"I'm afraid this is going to be a long call," Gen said very politely. "But I know there is another phone in that bakery across the street. I'm very sorry."

The woman smiled and nodded. "That's all right. Thank you for telling me."

"So what happened?" Ernest was asking. "Why won't she talk to you? Or maybe it's you who won't talk to her. No. No. She never said why, even though my sister keeps asking her. Oh! Okay. Now she wants to talk to you." Ernest held out the phone, and Gen took it.

"Hello—Mrs. Perl?"

"I just wondered what your mother told you when you asked why she was so angry with me."

"She didn't tell me anything. She just said she'd tell me when I was older. But I thought maybe you could tell us."

"No, dear, I can't. I think your mother is right. But . . . but . . ."

"Yes?"

"I just wondered if you would send me a picture of the two of you."

"Oh, sure. We've got lots. My father is a real camera nut. He's always taking pictures of all of us. I'll send you one he took of me in my Girl Scout uniform and one of Ernest on his bike."

"I hate that picture," Ernest said. "Send her the one of me swinging a bat."

"You can't see your face in that one."

"How about the one of me climbing up the flagpole?"

"No, because there's a big stain on your pants. Mom hates that picture."

"Well, I like it."

Mrs. Perl was laughing. "Send me any ones you like,"

she said. "And please call me again. Why don't you reverse the charges next time."

"Sure, Mrs. Perl, but when should we call you again?"

"How about Monday afternoon at the same time?"

"Okay."

"And Genevieve—"

"Yes?"

"Oh—nothing. Should I give you my address?"

CHAPTER TEN

By the end of the week, Gen's feelings toward Ernest had returned to normal. In spite of pleas and threats, Ernest continued to answer their phone in a number of obnoxious ways.

"Hello!" he might say. "This is Bishop's Bakery. Which crumb do you want?"

Or:

"Hello! This is Bishop's Mortuary. You kill 'em, we chill 'em."

Or:

"Hello! This is Bishop's Hardware store. If you have a screw loose, we'll fix it."

Ernest had done the Bishop's Mortuary routine when Ms. Carrera called to speak to Dad. Evidently she had not been amused. When Dad hung up, he said, still patiently but with a burr in his voice, "Ernest, you really have to stop answering the phone in that silly way."

"Why?" Ernest asked. "It's funny."

"Well, it's not funny to everybody. Ms. Carrera didn't think it was funny."

"I didn't know it was going to be Ms. Carrera," Ernest said.

"Well, that's just it," Dad said. "And your bit about Bishop's Hardware fixing loose screws. I don't think any of my customers would think that's so funny either. So, Ernest, I want you to stop. Ernest? Do you hear me, Ernest?"

"I hear you," Ernest said.

Ernest may have heard Dad, but he didn't stop. He just developed some new greetings.

"Hello! This is Bishop's Deli. Which sour pickle do you want?"

Or:

"Hello! This is Bishop's Zoo. Which skunk do you want?"

Life could have been so much sweeter, Gen thought, if she had been an only child. Maybe if Ernest had been a girl, not even necessarily like herself, but a normal girl with normal pleasures, that might have been okay, too. At times Gen wondered if all males were afflicted with a different, more primitive, set of genes. All through school, from nursery school up until the present, Gen had observed that boys made the most trouble. It was boys who made loud, disgusting noises, boys who disrupted classrooms, boys who were wild, uncooperative, silly, and puzzling. Some girls, she knew, acted up too, and some boys seemed sane and civilized, but usually it was the other way around.

By the end of the weekend, everything had returned to normal. Monday afternoon, when Gen called Mrs. Perl, Ernest was not even with her. He had been invited to remain after school in the principal's office for directing a drinking-fountain war against the second-graders.

"He's always in trouble," she explained to Mrs. Perl.

"Maybe he just went along with the other boys."

"No, it was his idea. He even admitted it. That's why Ms. Carrera, the principal, made him stay in her office this afternoon. It's always his idea."

Mrs. Perl sighed. "Well, I never had a boy. Your mother wasn't any trouble—as a child."

"I know," Gen agreed. "Dad keeps saying she was the nicest and the smartest and the prettiest girl in their school. You know he was in her class—oh yes, I forgot, you would know."

"Yes, I do know," Mrs. Perl said quickly. "And your father, he . . . well . . ."

"Oh, I know about him, too." Gen laughed. "He

keeps saying that Ernest is a lot like he was, and that Ernest will outgrow it the way he did."

"Your father says that?"

"Oh, yes. He admits he was wild and kind of bad when he was a kid."

"And now?" Mrs. Perl said carefully. "And now? I mean—what's he like, your father?"

"Oh, he's great, most of the time. You know, he and Mom own a hardware store."

"I know," said Mrs. Perl carefully. "I wish I knew more, but I'm not really in touch with too many people. Anyway, your mother—does she work there also? All the time?"

"Most of the time, now that we're in school. But if we're sick, she stays home with us. Now they have a couple of part-timers to help out, but Dad's in the store most of the time. I guess he works hard, but he hardly ever yells or loses his temper. Only once, last week, when he thought—well—Mom's the one who blows up. She really yells when she gets angry. Were you like that, Mrs. Perl? Did you yell, too?"

"Genevieve," said Mrs. Perl, "would you do me a favor?"

"Sure."

"Well, would you call me—Grandmother—or Grandma—just not Mrs. Perl."

"Okay," Gen agreed, "but then you have to call me

Gen, not Genevieve. Anyway—Grandma—did you yell a lot?"

"Certainly not, Gen. I don't think I ever yelled or even raised my voice. I'm surprised to hear your mother does. She never did as a child. But she was always very stubborn."

"She's still stubborn, and if she didn't yell, it was because she didn't have Ernest in her life then," Gen said grimly. "Do you know what he did to me yesterday?"

"What?"

"Well, I have this doll's house Dad made for me when I was seven. It's beautiful. He and Mom worked on it together. She made all the rugs and the curtains and the upholstery. And he made the furniture and put in lights. It has a little washing machine that chugs and a refrigerator that makes humming sounds."

"Your father did that?"

"Oh, yes, he's very handy. He made Ernest a whole little village for his model train set."

"I didn't know he was handy."

"Anyway, I don't play with the doll's house much anymore, but I love just having it all set up with everything in the right place. So yesterday, Ernest came into my room—he's always coming into my room when I'm not around and messing up my things—and he took away all the furniture and put up a FOR RENT sign outside the house. You should have heard me yell."

Grandmother Perl was thinking. "It is hard to understand boys," she said. "Nowadays they say boys and girls are just the same, but I never believed that."

"Neither do I, Grandma." Gen giggled. She liked saying *Grandma*. "Most of my teachers say that girls and boys are equal in every way, and that it's important for a girl to feel she can do anything a boy does. But I don't want to do most of the things boys do."

"Did you send me a picture of you and your brother, Gen?"

"Yes, I did, Grandma. I sent you three of me and two of Ernest. I mailed them on Saturday, so you should get them soon. When should I call you again?"

"How about Wednesday? I should have your pictures by then."

"I wish I had a recent picture of you, Grandma. I have an old one of you at a picnic when Mom was about my age. You're holding a chocolate-chip cake. We love that cake."

"Does your mom still make it?"

"Oh, sure, for all of our birthdays. It's our favorite. Only now, I can make it by myself. Ernest likes to help, but he sticks his hands in the bowl because he likes the batter so much."

"I'm glad you like the cake." Grandma's voice was shaky.

"Are you sure, Grandma," Gen said, "that you don't

want to tell me why Mom's not talking to you? Maybe I could fix everything up if I knew what happened."

"I'm sure, Gen. Good-bye, dear. I'll talk to you on Wednesday. Don't forget. And, Gen . . ."

"What?"

"Give my love to Ernest."

Later, at home, Gen took out the album with Grandmother Perl's picture in it. She was smiling in the picture and so was Mom. She looked happy and so did Mom. But for twenty-five years, Mom hadn't talked to Grandmother Perl—to her own mother. Why? Stubborn, Grandmother Perl said. Mom was always stubborn. She still was, and Gen felt scared. She knew she never should have called her grandmother. She knew Mom would be angry. She knew . . . no, she didn't know.

She quickly shut the album and put it away. Mom would never be so angry that she would stop talking to Gen, would she? No, of course not! No! That could never, ever happen whatever she did—could it?

CHAPTER ELEVEN

▪ ▪ ▪ ▪ ▪

Two of the girls in Gen's cooking club joined her at home to color eggs for the kindergartners' Easter egg hunt. Mom had taken Ernest for his swimming lesson, so they had the house to themselves.

"It's wonderful when your brother is out of the house," Jill said, pasting some purple iris seals on a bright green egg. "It feels like a normal house."

"That's because you're an only child," Andrea told her. "Ernest may be off the wall, but this is a normal house when he's here. My two brothers are always running around our place, yelling and getting into all my things, and my little sister is a pain, too. The only place I can go where it's quiet is the bathroom in the basement. And even there, somebody's always sure to bang on the door." She was using a wax pencil to create designs on her egg before dipping it into a bright pink dye.

Gen pasted multicolored paper sprinkles on her yellow egg and held it away critically. "I don't know," she said. "It looks kind of boring."

"Put a little blue around the center. Blue always improves yellow," Andrea suggested. She had finished at least a half-dozen eggs that nestled brilliantly in a basket filled with artificial grass.

"You're so quick," Jill said, "and your eggs are really beautiful." She reached for a cookie and leaned back in her chair. She looked around the kitchen and asked, "Where's your microwave?"

"We don't have one," Gen said. She smiled over the blue stripe on her yellow egg. It did look better.

"Do you think your parents would like one for their anniversary? Maybe everybody could chip in and buy them one, instead of getting them a lot of little, stupid presents they probably don't want."

"I think it's nice to get a lot of little presents—and they don't have to be stupid," Andrea said. She added her pink egg with white designs to her basket and picked up another hard-boiled egg. "Mmm, maybe I'll try to draw a bunny on this one and color it green and orange."

Gen took a deep breath. She felt happy to be sitting around the table in her kitchen with two of her friends, coloring Easter eggs and talking peacefully of this and that. It was so seldom she had the house to herself. Mom kept telling her to invite her friends over whenever she liked, and now that Ernest was taking swimming lessons every Monday, she would make sure to invite them on Mondays.

"It's only a little more than two months to go," Jill said, "till the party. Maybe we ought to look over the house and decide what to do about the furniture."

"What do you mean?" Gen asked.

Jill added a multicolored egg to her pile and stood up. "Well, you'll probably have to move some of the furniture out to make room for all the people. Let's take a look at the living room first."

"I wasn't planning to move out any of the furniture," Gen protested, as Andrea followed Jill out of the kitchen.

"I wasn't planning to move out any of the furniture," Gen repeated to them in the living room.

"Well, I guess you can push most of it against the walls," Jill said. "But you will have to take all the plants out and the TV and that china lamp."

"There are too many things in here," Andrea said, walking into the small dining room. "There's not going to be any room if people want to dance."

"Dance?" Gen cried. "Who's going to want to dance?"

"Well, don't people usually dance at an anniversary party? It's kind of like a wedding, isn't it?"

"My father doesn't dance," Gen said firmly. "I'm not planning on anybody dancing."

"Okay, but you'll still have to move some things out, like that little table with the toaster. You can move the dining-room table over here in front of the windows. And the chairs—well, I guess some of the grownups will want to sit on chairs. The kids can sit on the floor. Let's take a look at the bedrooms now."

Gen's friends wandered all over the house and finally stood out on the small deck outside the kitchen, overlooking the untidy yard.

"It would be nice if you had flowers blooming back here for the party," Andrea said. "By June, all sorts of things are blooming, aren't they? It's only the beginning of April now. You might be able to plant a few things."

"My parents never had time to do any gardening, and if they did, my brother would mess it up," Gen said, trying to explain the yard. "He and his friends are always digging holes or having water fights. But maybe I can get him to help me straighten it up before the party."

"Karen's mother," Jill said, "has the most beautiful lilacs. I think they bloom early in June."

Gen hesitated. She knew Jill was friendly with Karen, so she said carefully, "Karen hates me. I don't know why."

"Well, I don't know why, either," Jill said.

"I know she's your friend, so . . ."

"Not anymore," Jill said. "I'd rather be your friend. That's what I told her."

"But you could be my friend and her friend, too. I don't want you to think you have to choose."

Jill shrugged. "Forget about her. Anyway, have you worked out how you'll get your parents away from the house so we can get everything ready and have all the guests hidden?"

"My Aunt Beth came up with a good idea," Gen said slowly. "She and my uncle will offer to take them out for dinner. They can even say it's for their anniversary. They'll pick them up at about six and take them over to Cliff House for drinks. They can say they want to see the sunset before they go off to a restaurant for dinner. My aunt will tip off the manager, so when we call at about seven and ask for our father, he'll be ready. He'll make an announcement and say there's an emergency, and is there somebody in the place named Dan Bishop. Dad will jump right up. He won't be suspicious. I'll tell Dad that the toilet is overflowing, and he'd better come right home. That will give us over an hour to get all the decorations up, put the food on the table, and hide everybody."

"And move all the furniture," Jill added. "Well, it sounds perfect. An hour is plenty of time. Nothing can go wrong."

The girls returned to the kitchen and resumed work

on the Easter eggs. By the time Mom and Ernest came home, a magnificent pile of multicolored eggs lay stacked and ready for the kindergartners.

"Did you invite Grandma to the party?" Ernest wanted to know that Wednesday, just before calling Stockton.

"No, I didn't, and we're not going to!"

"Says who?" Ernest said. "I want to invite her. I already told you—that would make it a double surprise party."

"But it might not be the kind of surprise Mom and Dad would appreciate, stupid. Maybe it would make them angry. We still don't know why Mom's not talking to Grandma. We don't want her to be angry at us."

"It's not going to make Mom angry," Ernest insisted. "Let's invite her."

"Let's talk it over first."

"We just talked it over. I want to invite her, and if you won't, I will."

"No, you won't."

"Yes, I will. And you don't even have to be around. I have her number, and I can call her when you're not around—the way you called her last week when I wasn't around."

"You weren't around because you had to stay in Ms. Carrera's office after school, and Grandma was expecting to hear from us that day."

"Well, I'm going to invite her."

"You are such a pest."

"And so are you. Here, give me the phone."

"Grandma said we should call collect," Gen told him.

"Well, okay, but I'm going to call today. It's my turn. Let go, Gen, and get away! You're crowding me. And stop breathing on me. Oh—hello—Grandma—it's Ernest— yes—yes—and I want to invite you to a party. It's on June seventeenth—my parents' twenty-fifth anniversary. It's a surprise party. No, they don't know you're coming. That will be part of the surprise."

Gen put her fingers in her ears. She felt terrified. The party was slipping completely out of her grasp. Hordes of people she didn't even know would be coming, and now Ernest had even invited Grandma Perl. Maybe her parents would be so angry, they would just storm out of the house when they saw Grandma Perl and all the strangers they didn't know. Maybe they would blame her. Maybe they would say, "We trusted you, and you deceived us. We never thought you would do anything to make us miserable. You were our dependable child, our darling—but now we see that you're no better than Ernest."

Every day more and more things were spinning out of control. In her mind, she suddenly saw Karen standing all alone as she had outside the superintendent's office. She closed her eyes tight.

CHAPTER TWELVE

But she didn't need to worry about Grandmother Perl.

"It's very nice of you and Ernest to invite me, Gen," Grandma said after Ernest handed her the phone, "but I don't like to go where I'm not sure I'd be welcome."

"Oh!" Gen said, relieved.

"I wouldn't want to upset anybody."

"I wish you could come," Gen said, now that it was safe to express a wish that would not come true.

"Well, that's very sweet of you, dear, and of Ernest," Grandma said. "And I did receive the pictures. You're both such . . . knock wood . . . such nice-looking children. I think I'm going to frame the one of you in your Girl Scout uniform. You do look just like your mother when she was your age. And I like the one of Ernest on his bike. I'm going to frame that one, too. He's such a handsome boy. I don't know who he looks like."

"Everybody says he looks like my dad."

"I don't think so," Grandma said quickly. "Uh-uh!"

"I guess you don't like my father, do you?" Gen asked. "I guess that's the reason Mom isn't talking to you. I guess you didn't want them to get married."

Grandma didn't answer.

"My dad is wonderful," Gen said loyally. Grandmother Perl needed to understand that she had better not say anything mean about Dad. Grandmother Perl should not think she could make derogatory remarks about Dad and get away with it. "He's the nicest man in the world," she continued. "And he hardly ever loses his temper."

"But you should tell her how he hit me last week," Ernest shouted.

"Oh, shut up!" Gen shouted back.

The next afternoon, Ms. Carrera called Gen into her office and handed her a note to bring home.

It seemed to Gen, as she walked slowly home, that the note in her backpack was as heavy as a rock. Ernest! It was about Ernest. Ms. Carrera's notes home were never about her. Never to describe any of her accomplishments—her high reading scores; her successful organization of the Easter egg hunt for the kindergartners; her involvement in school affairs; her election as class president two years in a row.

Nothing she ever did seemed to make any difference in this world. All of her achievements were just accepted by her teachers and her family. She was simply "the darling," while Ernest made the world spin on its axis.

Tears were still on her cheeks when she arrived home, but Mom didn't notice. She was busy baking Ernest's favorite Rocky Road cookies. Gen handed her Ms. Carrera's note, and Mom read it out loud.

Dear Mr. & Mrs. Bishop,

Ms. Chu and I are very sorry that Ernest broke his collarbone when he fell off the slide this morning. I know the children in his class will be sending get-well cards to him. I also know how difficult it must be for him to lie still for the next few days.

Please tell him that we miss him and hope he recovers soon.

Sincerely,
Lucy Carrera

P.S. You might also mention that we hope he has learned doing somersaults on the slide is not a good idea.

"He's actually sleeping now," Mom said tenderly. "He fell asleep on the couch in front of the TV. I don't know when he last took a nap in the afternoon. Poor baby!"

Gen burst into tears.

"Oh, Gen," Mom said, "I know just how you feel. It's so hard to see him lying there, so quiet and so helpless."

"I hate him," Gen cried. "Everything good happens to him."

"What?"

"I never broke anything," Gen wailed. "I never even sprained an ankle. He's broken his finger twice and now his collarbone. Everybody thinks about him and writes notes about him. Nobody thinks about me. It's like I'm just boring."

"Gen! Gen!" Mom said. She put her arms around Gen and hugged her very tight. "How can you say such a thing? We're so proud of you. You're such a darling."

"I hate that word," Gen snarled. "I don't want to be a darling. I want to be interesting. I want to be—no—I don't want to be like Ernest. I don't know what I want to be, but I want to be interesting."

"You are interesting just the way you are. I can't believe you'd ever be jealous of Ernest."

"I hate him," Gen said. But then Mom made her sit down, eat some cookies, and listen to the many ways Mom and Dad felt proud of her, and how different people kept saying how exceptional she was.

"Like who?" Gen wriggled.

"People I hardly know," Mom said. "This customer came into the store just the other day and told me how jealous she was that I had a girl like you who was so thoughtful and admired."

"Who was it, Mom?"

"I forget her name, but she said her daughter, a girl named Karen, never did a thing around the house and always complained about everything. She said Karen can't get along with anybody and doesn't have any friends. Do you know her?"

"Who, Karen? Oh, Karen! Sure, I know her. But what did her mother want in the store?" Gen asked nervously.

"She's apparently a big gardener. She wanted some tools and a new pair of gardening gloves, and she asked me to order some other garden supplies. We're getting so many new customers, and they're all so friendly. I just hope that Dad can manage for the next week while I have to be home with Ernest."

Gen was still thinking about Karen's mother. "How could she say all those nasty things about her own kid—about Karen? She didn't even know you."

"Well, I hope you're not going to repeat what I told you."

"Of course I won't. But, Mom, don't you think it's

wrong to talk about your own kid like that? You would never talk about me like that, would you? Especially to a stranger."

"No, I never would, but then, I don't have anything bad to say about you anyway. Dad and I think you're wonderful—you know that."

Gen took a deep breath. "Listen, Mom, I can stay with Ernest afternoons when I come home from school, and on Saturdays too, if you want to help Dad at the store."

"I don't know, Gen," Mom said doubtfully.

"I don't really hate him," Gen said. "Not most of the time."

And for the rest of the afternoon, she even managed to be kind to him and read him one of his favorite Goosebumps stories when he woke up.

The next day, Gen watched Karen in the lunchroom, eating by herself. It wasn't easy, but Gen went over and sat down next to her.

"Karen," she said. "I want to talk to you."

"What about?" Karen said. She was a small girl with dull red hair, pale eyelashes, and green eyes. She narrowed her eyes now and glared at Gen.

What was she going to talk about? Gen wondered. All she could think of at the moment was how sorry she was for Karen and how terrible it must be to have a mother who said bad things about you to strangers.

"Well, I was thinking . . ."

"Good for you," Karen said nastily.

No, it wasn't going to be easy, and Gen struggled not to get angry. It wasn't important what she, Gen, felt. She wanted to say something that would make Karen feel better. That's what was important. "I was thinking . . ." She focused on the small girl next to her, and then it came. "I was thinking how you gave me pink flowers to take home that time I came to your house in second grade."

"Primroses," Karen said.

"What?"

"They were primroses—the flowers I gave you."

"They were pretty."

Karen shrugged. "They're easy to grow. They come in lots of colors. We have clumps of them all over our garden."

"You . . . you like to garden?" Gen asked.

"Oh, sure," Karen said. "We all like to garden in my family. Even my bratty sisters have their own plots, and . . ."

Gen was nodding and smiling as Karen spoke. Suddenly Karen stopped and looked at Gen suspiciously. "Why are you asking about gardening?"

"Well," Gen said, "our yard is such a mess, and my brother and I are giving an anniversary party for my parents, and I wonder—I mean—I could use your help."

"My help!" Karen repeated.

"Well, I wonder if you would come over to my house today or tomorrow or any day soon and tell me how to clean up our yard and turn it into a garden."

"It was always so easy for you," Karen told her. Both of them were sitting on Gen's deck, overlooking the messy yard. "Everything was easy for you. You were always the most popular kid in the class. Everybody liked you."

"You didn't like me," Gen told her. "You hated me."

"No, I didn't," Karen said. "Not really."

"Well, you said I was a goody-goody and didn't have an original idea in my head. Maybe it's true. But it always mattered to me what you thought. You always had interesting opinions, even if nobody agreed with you."

Karen looked embarrassed. Then she jumped up and said, "Well, it's my opinion we'd better get to work on your garden." She hurried down the steps, and Gen followed her. It had not been easy making friends with Karen, and it probably would not be easy staying friends, either. But it seemed very important for Gen to try.

First, Karen said, they had to clear away all the old toys, deflated balls, and bits and pieces of unidentifiable objects. Ernest was able to sit up now, and he sat on the deck overseeing their work.

"Don't throw that old wagon out," he yelled.

"Ernest, it's all rusty, and look, it only has three wheels."

"What are you doing with that shovel? I need it."

"Just until the party, Ernest. We'll put it away in the basement. Why don't you go watch TV?"

"Because you're throwing out all my things. You're not throwing out your things."

"What do you think, Ernest?" Karen asked in an astonishingly sweet voice. "Should we put some geraniums here? Or do you think daisies would look better?"

"Huh?"

Karen had brought a weed whacker with her, and the girls took turns using it. She also showed Gen how to fill up the holes.

"We can sprinkle some wildflower seeds over the ground, and if you keep watering it, some of them might even grow in time for the party. Ernest, once you're feeling better, maybe you could help with the watering."

"What's going on here?" Mom demanded when she arrived home.

"They threw out my wagon," Ernest yelled.

"Oh, Mom . . . we want to do some gardening. We're

going to plant some bushes and sprinkle wildflower seeds all over the ground."

"Here?" Mom asked. "In our yard?"

"Won't it be nice to have flowers, Mom?"

"Well, sure, but you know how Ernest and his friends like to horse around in the yard."

"Not anymore. Right, Ernest?"

Ernest remained silent.

"Ernest is going to help water the flowers," Karen said in her sweet voice. "Right, Ernest?"

"Oh, yeah—right. I'm going to help them when I'm better. I'm going to water the flowers."

"What?" Mom looked very suspiciously at Ernest and then at Karen.

"Oh, and Mom," Gen explained, "I want you to meet my friend Karen. She's showing us how to garden."

CHAPTER THIRTEEN

Karen no longer ate lunch by herself. She started coming over almost every day to work in the garden. Sometimes Andrea or Jill joined her, and after a while, nobody seemed surprised that she had become one of Gen's good friends.

Karen scattered wildflower seeds all over the ground and showed Gen and Ernest how to water them.

"It's like a real patch of wildflowers out in the country. You don't even have to worry about stepping on them. They're pretty hardy."

She brought over pots, and plants to put in them— geraniums, daisies, and primroses.

"These will grow even if you neglect them."

In a short time, a green stubble of plants began sprouting.

"I wonder if we should try to develop a little rock garden over near that broken fence," Karen suggested. "It's already higher than the rest of the yard. We could arrange a bunch of stones or bricks, and I could give you some good, easy rock-garden plants like sedum and ice plants. What do you think, Ernest?"

She was the only one of Gen's friends who could get along with Ernest.

"It's really strange," Mom said. "Her mother, Wendy, keeps telling me how she fights with her sisters all the time and doesn't do anything around the house without a knock-down, drag-out battle."

"Well, she certainly isn't like anybody else," Gen said, "but I'm glad she's my friend. And just look how she gets along with Ernest. None of my other friends ever do."

"I told her mother that, and she couldn't believe it. But—Gen—whatever you do, don't tell Karen what her mother's been saying about her."

"I don't think I like her mother," Gen said. "I don't think it's right for a mother to bad-mouth her own kid."

"Well, she's really very nice, and she didn't know you were going to become so friendly with Karen. Actually, Wendy and I have a lot in common. I might even have lunch with her on Sunday. It's so nice to have a woman friend. I guess I just haven't had time."

"Did you have friends when you were growing up in Stockton?" Gen asked.

"Oh, sure." Mom smiled. "Like you, I had lots of friends. It's wonderful having friends. We had a club, and each girl's mother made refreshments. I don't remember what else we did, but we sure ate a lot of good things."

"I bet you always had chocolate-chip cake when your friends met at your house."

"Lots of times we did," Mom said, still smiling, still remembering other times. "But sometimes we had lemon cake—or plum cake if it was summer. I loved that plum cake. I wonder if I have the recipe. And sometimes we had gingerbread with whipped cream, or even linzer tarts."

"Grandmother Perl must have been a pretty good baker."

"Oh, yes." Mom nodded, but then she narrowed her eyes at Gen. "Please don't start that again. I told you I don't want to talk about it, and I mean it!"

"What could it be?" Gen asked Karen. Karen had become such a good friend that Gen told her everything about Grandmother Perl. They were sitting on the deck, rest-ing, after arranging some large stones over in the corner of the yard for the rock garden.

"Well, it obviously has something to do with your father."

"I told you how she didn't want to admit that Ernest looked like him."

"Ernest *is* very cute," Karen said.

Gen rolled her eyes.

"But I don't think your mother would stop speaking to her just because she didn't think Ernest looked like your dad."

"No! No! They haven't been speaking for over twenty-five years. It has nothing to do with Ernest."

"She probably tried to stop the marriage. Maybe that's the reason."

"She's not in their wedding picture. I bet that's what it is."

"Why don't you ask her?"

"Did you try to stop my parents from getting married?" Gen asked Grandmother Perl next time they spoke.

"Yes, I did," Grandma admitted.

"And is that why Mom doesn't want to speak to you?"

It took Grandma a while, but finally she said, "No, that's not the reason. I can't say anything more. Please don't ask me. I . . . I . . . think I was wrong. Not in my opinion of your father, although it seems he's turned out okay. But in something else. I can't say what it is, but I think I was wrong."

"Well, why don't you just apologize to Mom if you were wrong?"

"It's not so easy, Gen. And I don't think she would listen. I think she hates me."

"I don't think she does, Grandma. She was telling me the other day how she had a club when she was a girl that met at your house sometimes, and how you baked different things—chocolate-chip cake sometimes—but also gingerbread and plum cakes and linzer tarts."

"She told you that? Oh, Gen, I'm so happy she remembers some of the good times back then, too."

"Grandma, why don't you try? Do you want me to talk to her? I could tell her that we've been calling you and that you're sorry. Maybe if I tell her, she'd even call you."

"No! No! Don't say anything to her. Let me think about it. I really want to see her again—and you and Ernest."

"And my Dad, Grandma? Maybe he was kind of wild, like Ernest, but he's grown-up now."

"Maybe I should write her a letter," Grandma said. "Maybe I should write to both of them."

"Let me talk to Grandma now," Ernest yelled. "You've talked long enough."

Karen's mother, Wendy Knipper, came back to the house with Mom on the Sunday the two of them had lunch together. Gen and Karen were planting ice plants and dwarf impatiens in the rock garden, while Ernest was watering the rest of the yard.

"Ernest, you're getting me wet," Gen screamed. "You're purposely turning that hose on me. Now, cut it out!"

"Who, me?" Ernest said innocently, flipping the hose back and forth.

"I think those pink geraniums need some more water, Ernest," Karen said in her sweet voice.

That's when Mom and Karen's mother appeared on the deck.

"Oh, there's Mom," Gen said.

"Where?" Ernest managed to turn his body around in such a way that Gen's face was suddenly blasted with water.

"You little creep," Gen yelled, grabbing the hose away from Ernest and turning it on him.

"Gen!" Mom screamed. "Be careful. You'll hurt him. He's not all healed yet. Gen!"

"I'll kill him," Gen said, watering Ernest as he sped away.

"I didn't do anything," Ernest yelled. "Mom, she's just picking on me for nothing."

"Put down that hose this minute!" Mom bellowed.

"He purposely turned the water on me," Gen protested, but she put the hose down and turned, dripping wet and sullen, to be introduced to Karen's mother.

"Well, Wendy, this is my son, Ernest, and my daughter, Gen."

Mrs. Knipper was grinning. "It's a pleasure meeting you, Ernest, and especially you, Gen. I've heard all sorts of wonderful things about you. I didn't even think you were human!"

"She's hardly ever like this," Mom apologized. "I don't know what got into her."

"Oh, please don't apologize," Mrs. Knipper said. "I feel right at home here. And there's Karen—my goodness, I can't believe my eyes. Is that really you, Karen, working away so hard?"

"No!" Karen said in a nasty voice that Gen had not heard in a while. "It's my clone."

CHAPTER FOURTEEN

Mrs. Knipper had a few suggestions to make about how the garden could be even further improved. She also offered to bring over cuttings of some other plants.

"All of a sudden," Mom said, "everybody has become so friendly. We've had that store for over twelve years now, and, of course, we always got along fine with our customers. But in the past couple of months, all sorts of people we hardly knew before suddenly seem to think we're great." She giggled. "Even you, Dan. You've become everybody's heartthrob."

"Oh, cut it out, Amy."

"Wendy thinks you're very good-looking, and Bonnie says she wishes her husband kept his weight down like you do."

"Who's Bonnie?" Gen asked.

"Bonnie Ewing—Jill's mother. She always seemed kind of snooty to me. I know they have plenty of money and live in that big house up on Laidley, but now she's always dropping by the store just to chat. And the other day, she invited me to go swimming with her over at Koret Center."

"And Jim—he asked me to play golf with him."

"Who's Jim?" Gen asked nervously.

"Jim Ewing, her husband. I told him I don't have golf clubs and don't really know how to play. But he offered to lend me some of his and teach me. What's happening to us, Amy?" Dad grinned. "Why are we so popular all of a sudden?"

"They're going to get suspicious," Gen told Karen. "My mom is really getting friendly with your mom. I hope your mom can keep a secret."

"I hope so, too," Karen said doubtfully. "But anyway, you'd better think about sending out invitations. Who did you say was going to handle it?"

"Andrea's dad. He runs a print shop, and he offered to do it. We still have about six weeks to go, though."

"Well, you're going to have to decide what to say on the invitation, and you should have a list of people you're going to invite."

Gen shook her head. "I thought it was going to be a

small party, but now it seems as if everybody I meet—even people I don't know—are expecting to come."

"You should get a list of people your parents like. That would be a good way to start."

"They'd be suspicious if I ask them."

"Get Ernest to do it."

"Oh, him!"

Ernest did ask them, and Gen did not think Mom or Dad were at all suspicious.

"Nobody else," Mom said sleepily, buttering a piece of toast.

"What do you mean, nobody else?" Ernest insisted. "I thought you liked a lot of people."

"Well, sure," Mom said, pouring her coffee, "I do like lots of people, but I haven't got time to really like anybody except for my own family."

"And Aunt Beth and Uncle Josh?"

"Oh, sure."

"And their kids?"

"Of course. But that's what I just said—my own family."

"But lately you've been hanging out with Wendy Knipper and Bonnie Ewing. Don't you like them?" Gen asked, trying to sound casual.

"Oh, sure. I really like everybody, but Ernest asked

me who I liked best in the world. How can you answer a question like that?"

"You like the mayor, don't you?" Ernest yelled. "You like the president?"

"Don't raise your voice to your mother, Ernest," Dad said mildly, "and please pass me a banana."

"It didn't work," Gen told her friends. Now that Ernest was taking swimming lessons again, Karen, Jill, and Andrea came every Monday to help Gen work on the party.

"Well, let's get the invitations worked out first," Jill suggested. "Do you have any ideas?"

"Well, yes. I thought just a simple invitation on red paper. They both like red."

"How about using their wedding picture?" Andrea suggested. "They did that when my father's Uncle Harry and Aunt Bea were married fifty years. They showed their wedding picture on the invitation and printed it on gold paper."

"I thought maybe a big white heart on the red paper, and . . ."

"You'll have to use silver paper," Jill said to Andrea. "This is their twenty-fifth wedding anniversary, so it has to be silver, not gold."

"Right!" Andrea agreed. "And then you could say something cute, like 'Shh! It's a secret.'"

"And then tell when the party is going to be held and ask them to RSVP," Jill said.

"My mother says to use her number," Karen said.

"But I wanted to use my Aunt Beth's number," Gen said.

"No! No!" Jill shook her head. "She lives in Novato. It's too expensive to call Novato. My mother says you can use our number."

"And the invitation should explain it's potluck," Andrea continued. "They can tell Jill's mom or Karen's mom what they plan on bringing."

"But my Aunt Beth . . ."

The girls worked out an invitation, and all Gen had to do was sneak her parents' wedding picture out of the house and hand it over to Andrea, who gave it to her father.

Ernest smiled as he handed the note from Ms. Carrera over to Mom.

"Now what?" Mom demanded.

Ernest shrugged.

Mom read:

Dear Mr. & Mrs. Bishop,

I'm happy to say that Ernest has done a wonderful job as the second/third-grade supervisor of the Clean Team for the past week. I must admit that I

*was somewhat doubtful when his classmates voted
him in, but his behavior has been exemplary, and
his work extremely effective. The second/third-grade
yard has never looked cleaner. I hope this represents a
new beginning for Ernest and for the rest of us.*

Sincerely,
Lucy Carrera

"I don't understand," Mom said. "What's all this about?"

"Every classroom sends a representative to the Clean
Team," Ernest explained. "And then a supervisor gets
elected from every two grades to tell the others what to
do. I was elected supervisor of all the second- and third-
graders, and I tell them how to clean up the yard and how
to make everybody in their class throw out their garbage."

"And . . . and . . . this is something you like doing?"
Mom asked.

"Oh, it's great!" Ernest said. "I might even get this
year's Clean Team Award, even though I just started, and
school's over in a month."

"How come you just got elected now, in May?" Gen
wanted to know. "What happened to the old second/
third-grade supervisor?"

"She moved, so they had to hold a special election,
and most of the kids voted for me."

Dad was really proud. "That is wonderful, Ernest,"
he said. "I think you just needed a job with some respon-

sibility. And it's great that so many kids voted for you. You might like to run for some other kind of office next year—like president of your class. Look at Gen. She's been president of her class for the second year now."

"I don't think so," Ernest said. "Garbage is really fun. I'm going to try to be supervisor of the fourth/fifth grade next year, but they'll probably elect a fifth-grader."

"You hear a lot about waste management nowadays," Dad said.

"I don't," Gen told him.

"It's a new field. Sort of in engineering," Dad continued dreamily. "Maybe Ernest will grow up to be an engineer."

CHAPTER FIFTEEN

■ ■ ■ ■ ■

Now time began speeding up for Gen. Only four more weeks to go. One afternoon Mrs. Ewing, Mrs. Knipper, and a woman named Mrs. Gillespie, whom Gen didn't know, gathered at Jill Ewing's house to address envelopes and send out invitations. Gen, Jill, and Karen were there, too.

Jill's house was large and beautiful. The garden was also large and impressive. It was tended by a professional gardener.

"I'll bring yellow and pink roses," Mrs. Ewing offered as she stacked a group of addressed invitations on her left side and reached for a new bunch.

"And I'll bring lilacs," said Mrs. Knipper, "and lots of red and white roses. And columbine if it's up. I wonder what dress your mother is going to wear, Gen. I could make her a corsage if I knew the color of her dress."

"Well," said Gen, "she has a green silk dress she used to wear to parties, but it doesn't fit her anymore."

"It would be good if she went out and bought a new dress," said Mrs. Ewing.

"She hardly ever buys new clothes for herself," Gen said.

"We'll have some wildflowers coming up in their backyard," Karen said. "The poppies are budding, and so are the cosmos. Maybe you can make a corsage out of them."

"I don't think wildflowers are suitable for a corsage, dear," Mrs. Ewing said kindly.

"I don't know why not!" Mrs. Knipper nodded approvingly at her daughter. "Karen has really done an amazing job on the backyard. She has wonderful taste."

"Oh, Mom!" Karen's face turned a happy pink.

"I must say she really transformed it."

"Oh, Mom!"

"I helped, too," Gen said, but nobody seemed to hear her.

"Nobody hears me," Gen complained to Grandma. "The invitation says, 'Shh! It's a secret!' And then it goes on to say 'Genevieve and Ernest Bishop invite you to a surprise party in honor of their parents' twenty-fifth wedding anniversary.' But nobody listens to anything I say, and nobody pays any attention to what I want. There will be mobs of people coming, and I don't even know what anybody's bringing. Mrs. Knipper and Mrs. Ewing are making all the decisions. And now that Karen is getting along so well with her mother, even she doesn't pay any attention to what I want. Nobody hears anything I say."

"Well, they certainly sound like very good friends. Your parents are lucky to have such good friends."

"And that's the funny part, Grandma. They never really had any friends before I decided to give them the party. Suddenly they have lots of friends. Some of them I don't even know—and some I don't even like."

"Friends are wonderful," Grandma said quietly. "I used to have lots of friends when your grandfather was alive and—your mother was home."

"I think I'll go shopping for a new dress," Mom said three weeks before their anniversary.

"Great!" Dad said. "What's it for?"

"Now, Dan," Mom said, "you know we have a special event coming up."

"Oh? What?"

"Come on, Dan. What's going to happen later this month?"

Dad wrinkled his forehead. Gen and Ernest looked carefully at each other.

Dad shook his head.

"You never remember anything, Dan. I told you that the Ewings invited us to a fancy dinner-dance for his sister and her husband when they come in from Dallas later this month. It's going to be at their private golf club and sort of semiformal."

"Semiformal?" Dad made a face.

"Oh, you won't have to wear a tux or anything like that. Your dark gray suit will be fine. But maybe I'll pick up a white shirt for you and a new tie."

"I hate ties," Dad said.

"You can knot it loosely," Mom said. "But I guess I need a new dress. And besides, Beth and Josh are taking us out for our anniversary. You do remember that, Dan?"

"Vaguely." Dad grinned. "But I'm not going to wear a tie for that."

Aunt Beth came on a Saturday and offered to take Gen and Ernest out for lunch.

"How come?" Mom wanted to know. "What's the occasion?"

"Just like that," Aunt Beth said. "I want to have them all to myself for a change."

"Both of them?"

"Oh, absolutely."

They actually did have lunch before going on to the party store. Ernest wanted to go to McDonald's and Gen wanted to go to The Pancake House. Nobody ended up satisfied, because Aunt Beth settled the argument by taking them to Mother's, which was closed for repairs. So they ended up going to Rock Island Pizza, which nobody liked.

"Better get lots of plates, cups, and napkins," Aunt Beth advised at the party store. "It sounds as if you're going to have a mob."

Ernest wanted to buy cups, plates, and napkins with a cartoony pattern of blue dogs, red cats, and pink elephants drinking champagne with lots of pink, red, and blue bubbles on a purple background.

"It's stupid," Gen told him. "And it's gross!" She preferred a silver anniversary motif of silver bells and colored confetti on a white ground.

"Bo-ring!" said Ernest.

Their discussion became louder. Aunt Beth finally recommended tossing a quarter.

"Heads!" said Ernest.

"Tails!" said Gen.

The quarter came up heads, and Gen immediately burst into tears. "Nothing is happening the way I want it to," she cried. "It was my idea, and nobody pays any attention to what I want."

"Oh, go ahead and buy your bo-ring bells," Ernest said. "But I get to pick the colors of the balloons."

Ernest picked every color balloon available, and Gen,

feeling charitable, let him also pick a paper string of Hawaiian dancers in brilliant grass-green skirts to hang across one wall. Aunt Beth selected a large, white, frilly paper bell that opened up and displayed a silver "25" in its heart.

"We can hang it over the table," she said. "And now I think we have everything worked out except for the flowers. But it sounds as if your friends and their mothers are handling the flowers."

"What about games?" Ernest wanted to know.

"Nobody plays games at an anniversary party, uh . . ."

Gen was going to add "stupid," but she found herself feeling unusually charitable toward Ernest and refrained.

CHAPTER SIXTEEN

■ ■ ■ ■ ■

"My mother's changed," Karen said. "She's becoming a human being."

"That's nice!" Gen pulled up some weeds around a clump of white impatiens. The garden was actually turning green. With only two weeks to go, some of the wildflowers were even opening up—orange poppies, pinks, and blue cornflowers.

"She keeps saying nice things about me. Even to me!"

"Mmm!" Gen leaned over to smell one of the pinks. It had a sweet, spicy perfume.

"You're used to it," Karen said, "but it's new for me. Yesterday I carried out the garbage, and my mom made such a big deal you'd think I'd just won the Olympics."

"My mom picked out a white dress." Gen smiled.

"With yellow buttons and yellow embroidery on the sleeves."

"White and yellow? Well, I'd better talk to my mom. Maybe we could use Mrs. Ewing's yellow roses for the corsage, with some cornflowers, if there are enough. This is so much fun, Gen. I think I want to have a flower shop when I grow up."

"My dad hated the dress, so she took it back, and then she brought home a sheer red dress with a tight show-through slip underneath. It's kind of sexy for a woman her age, but my dad likes it."

"Red? Well, we can't use the yellow or pink roses. Something white would be better. Don't worry. We'll think of something. Anyway, did you hear? So far, around fifty-three people say they're coming."

"Fifty-three!" Gen said bleakly. "Nobody told me. Where are we going to put them all?"

"And we still haven't heard from about fifteen or twenty others. My mom says she's been discouraging people from bringing babies, but some of them say they can't get a sitter."

"I don't know where all of them are going to fit," Gen complained to Grandma.

"Let me talk to her," Ernest cried. "I was supposed to talk to her first. Give me the phone!"

"Don't grab, stupid!"

"Hello, Grandma . . . oh yeah . . . I'm fine. Yes, Ms. Carrera thinks I'm doing a good job. No, I'm not getting into any trouble . . . but, Grandma, I want you to come to the party. Listen . . . I could even send you the bus fare if you don't want to drive, and I could meet you at the depot."

It was sickening how Ernest kept urging Grandma to come to the party. Gen had explained to him over and over again how Mom and Dad would probably be so angry if Grandma just showed up that it would spoil the whole party. He wasn't listening to her, either—like everybody else.

"All right now," she said sharply to him. "Give me the phone! Give it to me right now! Hello . . . Grandma? Well . . . as I was saying . . ."

"He is such a sweet boy," Grandma said softly.

"Not in person," Gen said. "Maybe over the phone."

"Imagine offering to pay my bus fare!" Grandma laughed. "What a boy he is!"

Gen hesitated. Then she said, "You said you were going to write a letter to my parents. Did you?"

"Well, no, I didn't. It's not easy writing after all these years, but I am going to think of something. I have to think of something if I want to see you and Ernest. Oh, I want to say, Gen, if you need any money for the party, I'd like to send you a check. I could send it care of one of those women who are helping out."

"No, Grandma, honestly, we don't need any money. Ernest and I paid for the party supplies, but people insist on paying for everything else."

"I'd like to do something for them," Grandma said.

"I think you should write them a letter."

Suddenly, with only a week and a half to go, Mom and Dad changed. They smiled more, spoke tenderly to both Gen and Ernest, and spent time cleaning the house. Usually neither Mom nor Dad had much time to wash windows or clean out closets. But suddenly both of them were washing windows and cleaning out closets. They were also scrubbing floors, vacuuming walls, and polishing furniture.

"Now I know they're suspicious," Gen said to Ernest after Dad applied some lemon polish to the top of the scuffed dining-room table.

"Mom's washing the shower curtain," Ernest said, shaking his head. "She never washed that shower curtain before."

"I'll bet big-mouth Mrs. Knipper told her," Gen said, watching Dad polishing the tabletop.

"Should we change the day?" Ernest whispered. "Make it a week later?" He grinned his mean smile. "Then they'd figure they made a mistake. Maybe they'd even feel bad, but the next week, they would really be surprised."

"It's too late," Gen said glumly. "All the invitations

have gone out, sixty-seven people say they're coming, and it's impossible to change anything. But I wanted it to be a surprise party. I wanted . . ."

Ernest grinned. "It's still going to be a surprise party."

"No, it's not," Gen yelled. "They obviously know—and the only people who are going to be surprised are you and me."

"They're going to be surprised," Ernest insisted. "You'll see."

The next day, Ernest brought home a note from Ms. Carrera. It was the last week of school, and Mom smiled as she opened it. "Did you win the Clean Team Award, honey?" she asked.

"Uh—no—not exactly," Ernest said as Mom read:

Dear Mr. & Mrs. Bishop,

I'm very sorry to say that Ernest has been relieved of his duties as second/third-grade supervisor for the Clean Team. While it is certainly true that Ernest was one of the most dedicated workers we've ever had on the team, his fervor for the job grew completely out of hand. Dumping Jeffrey Kaplan into one of the garbage cans because he refused to pick up some litter was against the rules of the Clean Team. Ernest said he was sorry, but that was only after he had been relieved of his duties.

School will be over at the end of this week. I'm sure we're all looking forward to our summer vacation. Let me wish the two of you great happiness in the future.

> *Sincerely,*
> *Lucy Carrera*

"Now what happened, Ernest?" Mom asked in a more normal voice.

"That Jeffrey's always dropping his food on the ground," Ernest said angrily. "And most of the time it's pieces of egg salad. He's always eating egg-salad sandwiches. I warned him lots of times, but he never cleans up after himself, so this time I just pushed him a little, and he fell over in the garbage can."

"Oh, well," Mom said, folding up the letter and speaking again in her unnaturally soft voice. "Poor Ms. Carrera! I'm sure she'll need a good rest over the summer."

"Did you hear how Ms. Carrera wished Mom and Dad great happiness in the future?" Gen said bitterly to Ernest. "I bet she's coming to the party, too."

"She better not," Ernest yelled. "I'll drop a load of garbage on her if she does."

The final countdown began.

Five days to go—There were actually clumps of flowers in different parts of the garden. It looked pretty good compared to how it had looked before.

Four days—The house was so clean, it was almost uncomfortable. Dad kept shaking crumbs out of the toaster oven, and Mom swept up after each meal.

Three days—Mom asked Gen if she needed any new clothes.

"Like what?" Gen asked.

"Oh, for the summer," Mom said vaguely.

"You mean like a bathing suit?"

"Well, sure," Mom said. "And maybe a pretty summer dress and shoes. We can go shopping soon. Maybe today, and maybe we'll also pick up a nice shirt and a new pair of shorts for Ernest."

Two days—Mom decided she needed new kitchen towels. The old ones, she said, looked ratty. She also wished she could change the linoleum on the kitchen floor. She was sorry she hadn't noticed before how stained and cracked it looked.

The day before—Gen and Ernest called Aunt Beth from an outside phone. She told them she was busy cutting up radish roses, carrot curls, cucumber wheels, and little zucchini and salami boats. She would keep all the veggies in an ice chest hidden in the trunk of the car when they came to pick up Mom and Dad. She told Gen not to be nervous. Then Gen called Mrs. Ewing and Mrs. Knipper, who seemed surprised to hear from her. Both of them said that of course everything was going fine. They had decided on a corsage of white roses from Mrs. Knipper's garden with silver ribbons for Mom, and a white rose boutonniere for Dad. They both told Gen not to be nervous.

Gen wandered into Ernest's room in the middle of the night and woke him up.

"I'm nervous," she told him.

"Whu—?"

"I'm nervous, Ernest. I'm not sure Mom and Dad are going to be happy with this party. They're exhausted from all the cleaning, and they spent a lot of money on clothes for all of us. Aren't you nervous, Ernest? Aren't you worried?"

"No," Ernest said.

"Well, I just wish it was over. I'm beginning to be sorry I ever came up with the idea. Ernest! Ernest! Are you asleep?"

Ernest did not answer, which meant that he was.

CHAPTER SEVENTEEN

When Gen opened her eyes on Sunday, June 17, the first thing she thought about was ice.

"We're not going to have enough ice," she told Ernest, who was sitting on the floor of his room, opening out the paper string of Hawaiian dancers. "And put that away, stupid. You'll make them suspicious."

Ernest shoved the dancers under his bed and stood up.

"Call up somebody with a car," he advised, "and tell them to bring some. Call Aunt Beth."

"No, no. She can't bring it over. She and Uncle Dan are picking Mom and Dad up. Maybe I'll call Mrs. Knipper."

Dad came huffing and puffing up the stairs. "Are you

kids ready for breakfast? Mom wants you to finish breakfast so she can mop the floor. Boy, am I bushed." Dad flopped down on Ernest's bed and smiled lovingly at both of them.

"Why are you so bushed?" Gen wanted to know. "It's Sunday morning, and you're not working today. Usually you're only bushed after you work."

"Well, I was up early, and I just lugged thirty pounds of ice from the store to put into the freezer."

"Why?" Gen almost shrieked. "Why did you have to lug thirty pounds of ice to put into the freezer?"

"Well, you never know when you might need it," Dad said, jumping up. "Now hurry up, Mom wants to mop that floor."

"She just washed it a couple of days ago," Ernest said.

"It got dirty again. Come on, get a move on!"

The phone did not stop ringing all day, but Mom and Dad made no effort to answer it. Of course, they were busy vacuuming, scrubbing, dusting, and cleaning out the refrigerator and stove. They didn't even make a fuss when Ernest utilized his latest telephone greeting.

"Hello—this is Bishop's Soap Factory. Which slime-ball do you want?"

Most of the calls were for Gen, to check on the time.

"Do you think one hour will be enough, Gen?" Andrea's father, Mr. Page, wanted to know.

"Well, my Aunt Beth said she's going to pick them up at a quarter to six. That will give us an hour and fifteen minutes for all we have to do. And then it will take them fifteen to twenty minutes from Cliff House."

"Do you need any extra chairs?"

"I think we have too many chairs, because my friends say I have to move some of them out of the rooms."

"Maybe I'd better bring six or seven more, just in case. You're going to have a lot of people, I understand."

"I'm not sure where we'll put them, except out on the deck, and that's pretty small."

Mom and Dad just kept working the whole day and never even commented on all the phone calls. Dad found the string of Hawaiian dancers under Ernest's bed.

"What in the world is this, Ernest?" Dad asked.

"I . . . I just like them," Ernest said, looking helplessly at Gen.

"He just likes them," she echoed.

Dad laughed. "I would have thought you were kind of young for this. Mmm!" He opened it out and shook it so the grass skirts on the dancers jiggled. "But I'd say you have good taste, my boy. You can pass it on to me when and if you get tired of it."

"I told you not to keep it in your room," Gen said after Dad and his vacuum disappeared into her room. "You were supposed to hide it with the other things down in the basement."

Ernest jiggled the dancers and grinned. "That's great the way he did it. Don't worry, Gen, he wasn't suspicious."

Gen knew that they were more than suspicious. Mom and Dad worked the whole day, cleaning every room in the house, putting fresh towels in the bathroom, shaking out the welcome mat outside the front door.

At five o'clock, they staggered off to take showers and dress.

Gen wandered through the sparkling house, and her thoughts were bitter. Nothing had worked out as she had wished. Nothing! She opened the back door and walked out onto the deck. Somebody—not her—had swept the deck. Somebody—not her—had painted the old, rickety deck chairs a bright yellow. They looked silly on the small rundown deck, and even the garden, which she had enjoyed so much over the past couple of months, seemed full of bald, empty spots.

"Gen," said Mom from behind her. "How do I look?"

Gen turned, and there stood Mom in her new red dress with silver sandals on her feet.

Silver!

Mom giggled and twirled around so the red sheer skirt billowed away from the tight underslip.

"Do I look all right?"

What should Gen say? Mom was forty-five and a little overweight. She had dark patches under her eyes, and her lipstick looked very bright. She had gone to the hairdresser yesterday, and her hair lay stiff and high up on her head. But she was smiling. Maybe she was happy, even if the party was not going to be a surprise.

"Oh, sure, Mom. You look wonderful."

"Well." Mom giggled again. "I don't feel like me. I never dressed this way. Even when I got married, I wore just a simple outfit. This dress is way too young for me, but your dad insisted."

Then Dad came out onto the deck. Gen hardly ever saw him wearing a suit and a tie, but she knew he looked good—very good. Few of her friends' fathers were so trim and good-looking. Funny how she had never noticed before.

"Amy, you look like a dream," Dad said, shaking his head admiringly.

"You don't think it's a little too . . . too . . . youthful?" Mom asked.

"I don't," Ernest said, also coming out onto the deck. Gen thought nervously that even though there were only four of them on the deck, it already felt crowded. She wondered what was going to happen when the sixty-seven guests arrived. It did not seem possible that sixty-seven people could possibly fit into their small house.

"You look beautiful, Mom," Ernest said.

"My sweet boy!" Mom reached out an arm and pulled him over to her. She kissed his head, and then she kissed it some more. "And my darling girl!" Mom reached out the same arm toward her, and Gen stood up and began moving over. She noticed that Mom's fingernails were painted a bright red, and that on one of the fingers there was a small, unfamiliar diamond ring.

"I'm so lucky," Mom said, holding both Gen and Ernest very tight. "I have the most wonderful children in the whole world."

"What's that ring you're wearing, Mom?"

Mom looked very lovingly at Dad. "You tell them, honey."

"Oh, it's no big deal," Dad said. "I just gave it to her because when we were married, we didn't have any money, and . . ."

"Just enough to buy the license," Mom cut in. "But go on, Dan, go on."

"So—I just thought—listen, she's put up with me for twenty-five years, I'd surprise her with something she should have had twenty-five years ago."

"It's sexist for a man to give a woman an engagement ring," Gen said severely.

"Well, whatever it is," Mom said, breathing on it and holding it out, "I love it."

"It's very small," Ernest said, bending over it.

"No," Mom said. "It's just the right size."

As soon as their parents left, Ernest and Gen hurried upstairs to dress. The phone kept ringing, so it took much longer than it should have. Ernest couldn't find a clean pair of socks, and Gen's yellow headband that matched her new dress snapped, and she had to wear a white one. But, finally, they were ready.

"Your face is dirty," Gen scolded, "and your hair's not combed."

"Nobody's going to notice," Ernest said.

Gen grabbed him, dragged him off to the bathroom, and made him wash his hands and face while she combed his hair.

They stood looking at each other.

"You don't look like you," Ernest said. "You look good."

"So do you," Gen told him. The doorbell rang. The party was about to begin.

CHAPTER EIGHTEEN

∎∎∎∎

Where to put the chairs?

Mr. and Mrs. Page came early with Andrea, carrying six folding chairs. Then Mr. and Mrs. Ewing arrived with Jill and four more chairs. They decided to put a few out on the deck and the rest down in the garden.

"It's such a mild night," Mrs. Page said, stepping on a clump of lupine. She sniffed the air. "Just look at that blue sky."

But nobody had time to look. Guests were arriving in a stream, carrying pots and dishes and bowls of food.

Mrs. Shori asked if she could use the oven to heat up her tamale pie. But then Mrs. Uchida said she needed the oven too, and so did a bunch of other people. Mr.

Robbins, Gen's former teacher, said he didn't need to heat up his pesto sauce, but he knew Ms. Carrera would want to start boiling water for the linguine.

"Ms. Carrera *is* coming," Gen managed to whisper to Ernest, who looked grim. "Now, you just remember this is a party. You don't want to spoil it for Mom and Dad. Ernest, do you hear what I'm saying?"

"I hear," Ernest said. "But don't expect me to be nice to her."

"She's your guest, so you'll have to smile and say 'Hi' to her like you do to everybody else."

The noise grew deafening. Groups of people were moving furniture back and forth. Others were hanging up decorations and putting dishes on the table. Mr. Knipper carried in two large ice chests for the drinks and began burying them under the ice Dad had packed into the freezer.

All around her, people were hurrying back and forth, appearing perfectly at home in her house. Nobody seemed to need her advice or her directions. She stood in the middle of all this movement and almost felt as if she were in the way.

"What do you think of the corsage?" Karen asked, holding it up.

Gen took a deep, happy breath—somebody was finally talking to her. "It's beautiful," Gen said, looking at the small, delicate white roses nestling inside their silver ribbons.

"And here's the boutonniere for your father."

"Put it in the refrigerator," Mrs. Knipper suggested. But it turned out that there was no room in the refrigerator, with all the desserts and salads.

Most people brought gifts wrapped in fancy paper and tied with bright bows. They stacked them in a pile on one side of the dining-room table.

"We forgot to get them a present," Gen told Ernest.

"Well, we're giving them the party, right? Isn't that a present?"

"In a way, I guess. But we should have given them a real gift. Everybody else has. And—at least—we could have gotten them a card."

"Oh, no! Here she is. I'm getting out of here. And don't call me!" Ernest disappeared just as Ms. Carrera arrived, carrying two large bags. The tops of linguine packages stuck out of one.

"Hello there, Gen," Ms. Carrera said. "Isn't this exciting? I'm so glad you and Ernest invited me. Gil has been talking about nothing else for weeks."

"Gil?"

"Gil Robbins. He makes a wonderful pesto sauce, and he decided, since I'm not much of a cook, that I'd better make the linguine. Oh, there he is. Hi, Gil."

"Hi, Lucy. Did you remember to bring a big pot? Somebody is using the Bishops' pot to make spaetzle."

"I remembered."

"Good girl!" Mr. Robbins, who was at least in his fifties, bald and overweight, smiled approvingly at Ms. Carrera, who was also in her fifties and overweight, but not bald.

Gen was astonished. She watched as Mr. Robbins helped Ms. Carrera find an empty spot to set down her bags, and noticed how his hand rested for a long minute on her shoulder.

She moved out into the hall, and Ernest peeped out of the hall closet. "Where is she?" he whispered.

"She's in the kitchen with Mr. Robbins," Gen said. "I think they're in love with each other."

"Nobody can be in love with Ms. Carrera," said Ernest, coming out of the closet. "Who invited her anyway?"

The doorbell rang again as it had been ringing over the past half hour. More and more people arrived with more and more coats and jackets.

"There's no more room in this hall closet," Mrs. Ewing said, looking around. "Don't you have another closet down here?"

"No," Gen said. "There's one in my parents' room, and one in my room and in Ernest's."

"Well, maybe you and Ernest and Jill could take all the extra coats and jackets and just lay them down on Ernest's bed."

"Why in my room?" Ernest wanted to know as they were carrying up a bunch of coats and jackets.

"Because that's what she said," Gen told him.

"Well, why didn't she ask me?"

"Okay! Okay! We'll put them on my bed. You make a fuss over nothing."

"So do you. And I didn't say not to put them in my room, did I?"

They put all the coats in Ernest's room, and that's when he remembered the string of Hawaiian dancers under his bed. "I forgot all about them," he said. "Let's go hang them up."

Both Mrs. Gillespie and Mrs. Ewing said they didn't think Hawaiian dancers were appropriate for an anniversary party, and besides, there wasn't any room for more decorations.

Gen looked around the mobbed living room and the packed dining room. Two clumps of helium-filled balloons rose colorfully up to the center of each ceiling. Aunt Beth's white and silver bell hung from silver streamers over the dining-room table, and somebody had strung up HAPPY 25TH ANNIVERSARY, AMY & DAN on the wall in the living room.

"There's simply no room, dear," Mrs. Ewing said patiently. "I think everything looks just wonderful exactly the way it is."

"And besides, those dancers are—well—not appropriate for an anniversary party," said Mrs. Gillespie.

"I want them up," Ernest insisted in a loud voice. "I like those dancers, and so does my father."

Gen could see his ears turning red, and she clenched her fists and prepared to intercede. But then somebody else spoke up in a firm, no-nonsense voice.

"I think if Ernest wants to put up the dancers, that's his privilege. After all, he and his sister are really giving this party."

It was Ms. Carrera. Nobody contradicts a principal, so in a short time, the string of Hawaiian dancers jiggled around in the doorway between the living room and the dining room.

"Maybe I won't throw any garbage at her," Ernest said. He looked at his Mickey Mouse watch.

"How much more time have we got?" Gen asked.

"For what?"

"For when I'm supposed to call."

"Oh, right! I guess in about twenty minutes."

In twenty minutes, most of the guests had arrived. They packed all the downstairs rooms, spilled out onto the deck, and stood on the steps leading down to the garden. In the kitchen, people bumped into each other as they tried to assemble platters and bowls of food. In the bathroom and upstairs bedrooms, parents diapered infants and nursed babies. But everybody seemed cheerful and polite.

"A few people aren't here," Mrs. Knipper said impatiently. "But I guess we should start."

"Oh—" said Mrs. Ewing. "Did all of you remember to park at least a block away? We don't want them to see a whole bunch of cars in front of their house."

"There's no place to park on this street, anyway," a man grumbled.

Mrs. Knipper looked all around the assembled group and announced in a very low voice, "Now here's the plan. Gen is going to call her father at Cliff House. Dan and Amy are having drinks there with his sister and her husband. She's going to say that the toilet is overflowing. Then we'll have fifteen minutes until they get back. I guess we can put out the lights after ten minutes, and, Luke," she told her husband, "you stay near the window and tell us when they drive up. Is everybody ready? Okay, go ahead, Gen!"

Gen picked up the phone and dialed the number. She felt totally calm and in control. There would be no surprises. Her parents would not be surprised. The manager of Cliff House would not be surprised. Nobody would be surprised.

The phone rang and rang and rang.

"Nobody's answering," she announced.

"They're very busy, especially over the weekend," Mrs. Page said. "Just let it keep ringing."

The phone rang and rang and rang.

"Nobody's answering," Gen said, surprised. "Why isn't anybody answering?"

CHAPTER NINETEEN

▪ ▪ ▪ ▪ ▪

Nobody was answering because Gen had the wrong number. Ernest figured it out before anybody else did. Gen tried again. The phone rang only three times before somebody picked it up.

"Cliff House," said a man's voice.

"This is Genevieve Bishop. I think my parents are . . ."

"Oh, right! Just hang on a minute!"

Genevieve turned and nodded to all the guests, who were silently watching her. She held the receiver very hard against her ear and heard a loud man's voice in the distance making some kind of announcement. That's when a sudden fit of giggles overtook her.

"Hello!" came Dad's voice over the phone.

"Oh . . . Dad . . . oh . . . hello . . . oh!" Suddenly Gen could not say another word. All she could do was giggle.

"Stop it! Stop it!" Mrs. Ewing hissed.

Ernest grabbed the phone away. "Dad . . . Dad . . . listen, the upstairs toilet's overflowing . . . all over the floor . . . yes . . . yes . . . I did . . . but it's just making it worse. No . . . no . . . I can't stop it. It's coming through the ceiling. You'd better come right home. . . . Hurry up . . . no, she's fine . . . she's just very upset. . . . Hurry!"

Ernest hung up and turned, grinning, to all the assembled, smiling guests. "He fell for it," he announced.

"Good job, Ernest!" Mrs. Ewing nodded approvingly. Then she turned to Gen. "What happened to you? You nearly messed it up."

Gen did not answer. She had stopped giggling by now and was feeling ashamed and humiliated.

"It's a good thing Ernest used his head," said Ms. Carrera.

"Well, let's not just stand around," somebody said. "They'll be coming back soon, and we'd better get ourselves ready."

Ernest looked at his watch.

"How much time do we have, Ernest?" Mr. Robbins asked.

"Oh, right . . . about ten, fifteen minutes. I guess

some of you could stand on the stairs going up to the bedrooms, and maybe some of you should move into the kitchen."

Ernest began directing the traffic, and everybody seemed to respect his opinions. Gen tried to fight down a heavy, unhappy feeling rising up from her feet. How could she have messed up? What was wrong with her, anyway? She wanted to run away and lock herself up in the bathroom. But then she caught sight of herself in the hall mirror—a dark-haired girl in a lovely, yellow-flowered dress. The girl was scowling, but she looked so pretty, Gen had to make her smile. So what if Ernest had finally done something right for a change? She knew it wouldn't last. And really, she was the hostess of this surprise party, even if it really wasn't a surprise and others had taken over her responsibilities. It was still a party, wasn't it?

"Okay—maybe some of you can stand here in the dining room, away from the window. Just make sure to leave room in the hall so they can come through the door," she suggested, feeling better and more important.

She and Ernest began moving people into the different rooms, and then out of them as they became too crowded. Everybody was laughing and talking and trying to put dishes of food on the dining-room table or into the refrigerator. A lively discussion arose about whether or not to put out all the lights in the house. Mr. Shori thought yes, but Mrs. Ewing thought no.

"They gave my brother-in-law a surprise party for his fiftieth birthday," she said solemnly. "And they put out all the lights. But he got so scared when he came into the house that he had a heart attack and had to be rushed to the hospital."

"No, no, Mom. He had to go to the hospital after the party, because he ate so much lasagne and chocolate fudge cake. It wasn't because he was scared."

Everybody had an opinion, but finally Ernest said, "It won't be a surprise if you don't put out all the lights. They'll be able to see people from the living-room windows before they even get into the house. You have to put out all the lights!"

He looked at his watch. Gen looked at hers, too. "They'll be here in another five minutes or so. I don't think they'll be . . . I mean . . . I don't think either of them will have a heart attack, so let's put out all the lights and try not to talk so loud," she advised.

All the lights were put out, but a little light still shone in from the street. Gen found an empty spot on one of the middle steps, and Ernest came and sat down next to her.

"It's not really going to make any difference whether the lights are on or off," she whispered to him. "They're not going to be surprised whatever we do."

"Oh, they'll be surprised," Ernest said.

"How can you say so, Ernest? You know they've been cleaning the house for weeks. They never clean the house. Of course they know, but I guess they like the idea."

"They're going to be surprised," Ernest insisted. "You'll see."

"Shh!" People began whispering that everybody else should shut up. Suddenly it grew very, very quiet. Gen could see shadowy shapes almost everywhere she looked. It seemed a miracle that so many people could fit into her small house.

"Luke! Luke!" Mrs. Ewing whispered. "Do you see anything yet?"

"No."

"Well, maybe they'll come up Church Street. Are you looking both ways?"

"Of course, I am. Wait . . . wait . . . here comes a car. It's slowing down . . . oh! . . . it's . . . no . . . it's passing the house. What kind of car does your uncle drive, by the way, Gen?"

"Oh, it's kind of a tan car."

"A Toyota Camry," Ernest said. "Four-door sedan."

Gen barely had time to be irritated when Mr. Ewing whispered, "Okay! Okay! I think this is it . . . yes . . . it's pulling into the driveway . . . Dan is jumping out of the car. He's hurrying up the stairs . . . and . . . good . . . good, Amy's right behind him. Everybody—freeze!"

Nobody moved. It seemed as if nobody breathed as they listened for Dad's key in the lock. They could hear Mom's voice, but it wasn't clear what she was saying. Then the door opened, and Dad called out, "Gen! Ernest! Where are you?"

Somebody flipped on the hall light, and sixty-seven voices screamed out, "Surprise!"

Gen looked at her parents standing there, blinking in the light. Mom's makeup was not at all blurry. Dad's hair was combed, and, yes, he was wearing the new tie that he had said he would not wear. They were smiling and pretending to be surprised, but Gen knew they were not surprised.

"See!" she said to Ernest. "I told you they wouldn't be surprised."

But he was jumping up and down on the step, hollering "Surprise! Surprise!" louder than anybody else.

CHAPTER TWENTY

■ ■ ■ ■ ■

Mom and Dad played along with being surprised and were so good at it that nobody except Gen suspected. Even Ernest seemed to be caught up in all the loud greetings and questions.

"You really were surprised, Dan?"

"Oh, absolutely!"

"Even when Gen had that fit of giggles over the phone, Dad? Weren't you suspicious then?"

"But you said she was upset. So that's what I thought."

Then Ernest started acting like he was the emcee. He carried two glasses of champagne over to Mom and Dad and began yelling again, "Surprise! Surprise!"

"Stop saying that!" Gen told him. "You keep saying

that, and the surprise is over." Ernest grinned and looked at his watch. That's when the doorbell rang again.

"I'll get it!" Ernest lunged for the door. He opened it, and a giant rabbit stood outside.

"Is this the domicile of Mr. and Mrs. Daniel Bishop?" asked the rabbit in a deep, penetrating voice.

"It sure is," Ernest said, flinging the door open as wide as he could.

The rabbit entered. "Who in this magnificent company are Mr. and Mrs. Bishop? I have an important message for them."

"You have to guess," Ernest yelled, leaping around the rabbit. "Are you supposed to be Bugs Bunny? Is that pink thing back there supposed to be your tail?"

"Don't be impertinent, young man," said the rabbit. "Unless you, perhaps, are Mr. Bishop."

"Yes, I am Mr. Bishop," Ernest said.

Everybody laughed. Mom and Dad, holding their champagne glasses, laughed too.

"Ah—and Mrs. Bishop?"

This went on for a while until the rabbit explained that he had a telegram from Uncle Joe, Dad's brother, in Germany. The rabbit sang the message in a booming baritone, wishing them a happy anniversary and regretting that Uncle Joe and Aunt Lisa could not be there to celebrate with them.

The rabbit lingered for a while and danced with

Ernest, with Mom, and even with Mr. Ewing. He was invited to remain and join the party, but he said his boss, Farmer McGregor, would turn him into a scarecrow if he did.

"How did you know he was going to be coming?" Gen asked Ernest after the rabbit left.

"I didn't," Ernest said.

"But you acted like you did," she insisted. "I saw the way you answered the door when you heard the doorbell. Is that why you kept saying Mom and Dad were going to be surprised?"

"There it goes again," Ernest yelled, springing over to answer the door. This time it was Mr. and Mrs. Jensen, who said they were late because they couldn't find a parking spot.

Somebody proposed a toast. Champagne bottles popped, and all the guests held up their glasses.

"To Dan and Amy! Here's to twenty-five more!" said Mr. Ewing.

"To Dan and Amy!" everybody echoed.

Then Dad made a speech saying how lucky he and Mom felt to have so many good friends and such wonderful kids.

Mom reached out her arms to both Gen and Ernest and hugged them tight. She held up her glass and said, "Now I want to propose a toast. I want to wish all of you the greatest happiness in your lives, and I want to thank you for giving us this wonderful surprise party. I'll never forget it as long as I live."

Then the party really began. Everybody suddenly was starving, and everybody tried to move into the dining room where the food was crammed onto the table—so many different kinds of dishes that Gen stood there blinking, bewildered by so many choices.

"Try my mother's chicken salad," Karen said, pointing to a large bowl. "It's really great."

Karen was wearing a shiny blue dress and had fastened some blue cornflowers in her red hair. "What a party! I never saw so much food in my whole life, did you? And what do you think of the flower arrangement my mom made? Isn't it gorgeous?"

"Please give me a little room. Please. Make some room on the table. Gen, could you just make a little space for us."

Mr. Robbins was carrying a huge dish, filled with a vast quantity of pesto pasta. Ms. Carrera followed behind, holding a big bowl of grated cheese.

Mom rested a hand on Gen's shoulder. "You are such a darling, Gen, to have planned this for us. I just can't believe so many people wanted to get involved."

"Is it all right, Mom?" Gen asked in a low voice. "You really don't mind having this mob of people?"

"Oh, no," Mom said, her cheeks very pink. "I love it."

Dad said the same, and it did seem to Gen that in

spite of all the people and all the noise and a few screaming babies and some food dropping on the floor and one
of Ernest's friends falling down the stairs, everybody—
including her parents—was enjoying themselves.

She, Karen, and Jill pushed their way out onto the
deck. The night was so mild, nobody needed a coat. The
stars were big and bright, and there was a sweet smell
from downstairs.

"Let's go down to the garden," Karen suggested.

The girls carried their plates down the stairs and sat
on some of the extra chairs. Gen could hear a guitar suddenly and voices singing.

"Mmm! This pesto pasta is delicious," Karen said.

"What do you think of Ms. Carrera's dress?" Jill
whispered. "It's pretty low in the front, don't you think?"

"Is Gen down there?" Ernest called down from up on
the deck.

"Yes. What is it?"

"You'd better come up here. Fast! Hurry!"

"What's wrong?" Gen put her plate down on her seat
and hurried up the stairs. "What's happening?"

"The car's pulling in front of the driveway."

"What car?"

"I guess it's a Plymouth—maybe a few years old."

"Ernest, what are you talking about?"

But he was hurrying away, and she followed him
through the kitchen and dining room into the narrow

hall. Gen could see both her parents sitting on the couch in the living room, surrounded by their friends. Her parents were laughing. Obviously, they were enjoying their party—surprise or not.

"What is it, Ernest?"

The doorbell rang. Again Ernest lunged to open it. No rabbit this time. Only a small, thin, gray-headed woman standing there, smiling nervously. She was holding something in her hands.

"Come in! Come in!" Ernest said.

"Are you . . . Ernest?" asked the woman.

"Yes, and this is Gen."

"Gen!"

The woman took a few careful steps just to the threshold and stood there, waiting.

"Mom! Dad!" Ernest yelled. "It's for you."

"Another telegram?" Dad said, laughing. He and Mom eased themselves up from the couch and, smiling, worked their way toward the door.

Do something! Gen thought. Say something. But nothing occurred to her. She just knew that now the party would be over. Ernest had ruined everything, as he generally did.

She watched her parents' faces as they moved closer and looked at the woman in the doorway. She watched Mom's face as her smile faded.

"Amy," said the small, thin woman in the doorway.

"Amy," said Grandmother Perl. "I'm sorry, Amy." Then she looked beyond Mom to Dad. "And Dan. I'm sorry. I was wrong. I did a bad thing, and I want to apologize. I should have said so years ago. Will you let me come in?"

Only the group standing at the doorway was silent. All around them the sounds of the party continued— laughter from the living room, the guitar on the deck, a champagne cork popping . . .

Mom was the first to break the silence. What was she saying? Gen turned, and saw Mom put her hands up to her face and begin to cry. That's when Dad stepped closer. "Please come in, Mrs. Perl," he said. "We're glad you came."

CHAPTER TWENTY-ONE

"Let's find a place to talk," Dad said.

But where? There wasn't an inch of space anywhere.

"Down in the basement," Ernest suggested. "Nobody's down there."

Dad flipped on the lights before they made their way down the steep, creaking steps. They all heard a noise, and Dad called out, "Is anybody down there?"

"Uh—it's only—Lucy and me," said Mr. Robbins, blinking up from the bottom of the stairs. "We were trying to . . . to . . . see if there was any more ice down here."

"It's all upstairs in the freezer," Dad said.

"I should have thought of that," said Mr. Robbins. "Come on, Lucy, let's go find some."

"Did you notice Mr. Robbins had lipstick on his

head?" Ernest said, after the two of them had squeezed past.

Suddenly Mom was laughing.

"Mr. Robbins," Dad explained to Grandma Perl, "was Gen's teacher last term, and Ms. Carrera is the principal of their school."

"She used to hate me, Grandma," Ernest said, "like I told you. But I don't think she does anymore."

"I don't understand," Dad said. "What do you mean, Ernest, about telling . . . uh . . . Mrs. Perl?"

"Let's go downstairs," Ernest said. "We can go sit on Dad's workbench. Watch your step, Grandma, that last step's shaky."

Grandma Perl began explaining even before the five of them arranged themselves against the workbench. "The children called me. I don't know why. For years I tried to think of a way I could make it all change, but I didn't know how. When your father was alive, Amy, he wanted me to apologize to you, but I was too proud . . . and too angry. Then he got sick. I should have called you then and told you to come."

Mom started crying again. "I would have come," she said. "I didn't know he was sick."

"But even then, I couldn't think right, and it all happened so fast. Afterward, nothing was right. I was so miserable and unhappy and I was angry at you—at both of you—but most of all, I know, I was angry at myself. And then the children called."

"But why?" Dad wanted to know, looking at Gen. "Why, all of a sudden, did you call?"

"I wanted to call," Ernest said. "I looked up her number, and I made Gen call."

"You didn't make me call," Gen insisted. "I wanted to call her, too."

"It was my idea," Ernest said. "And it was my idea for her to come to the party. Gen said no."

All of them were looking at her. Gen wanted to explain how she thought Mom would be angry and how it would spoil the party, but then Grandma said, "And then Ernest said he would pay my bus fare and that he would meet me at the depot. Nobody, since your father died, Amy, nobody said anything so nice to me in all that time."

"But Grandma said no."

"And then . . ." Grandma put her package down on the workbench and pulled a tissue out of her purse. Now she was crying, too. She patted her eyes. "And then . . . he sent me the money."

"You never told me you did that," Gen said.

"Because you would have said no."

"And then he started calling me, so I said yes, I would come, but I would drive. And I told him when to look for me."

"See!" Ernest said, grinning at Gen. "I told you it was going to be a surprise for them. It was even a surprise for you."

"He is quite a boy," Grandma said. "And now that I see him in person, Dan, I do think he looks like you."

"Yes, he is quite a boy," Dad agreed.

"And Gen!" Grandma said. "She's just like you, Amy, when you were young and—"

"And thinner," Mom said.

Grandma took a deep breath. "I did a very bad thing to your parents, children."

"It's all over," Mom said. "Let's not talk about it. I'm . . . I'm glad you came, Mother. It's enough that you came."

"No, it isn't," said Dad. "I want Ernest and Gen to know what happened, because then they can understand why I was so angry a couple of months ago when Ernest was accused of stealing money from his teacher's desk."

"Ernest!" Grandma said sharply.

"It was a mistake. He didn't do it," Dad said quickly, "but I thought he did, and I was very angry. I did a bad thing, too. I didn't let him explain—and I hit him. It was terrible. Anyway, now I can tell you, Ernest and Gen, it was because I got into a lot of trouble when I was a kid. I stole things, and . . . and . . . I was even sent away for six months when I was seventeen. I didn't want the same thing to happen to Ernest."

"But then it was all over," Mom said quickly. "When he came back, he really had changed. He worked hard at a hardware store in town, and he never ever stole anything again. Never!"

"I knew he was trying," Grandma Perl said, "but I didn't trust him. And Amy—I only had you—and you were such a good girl and such a good student. Your father and I wanted you to go to college and make something of yourself."

"I have made something of myself," Mom said sharply. "Dan and I have both made something of ourselves."

"I'm sure you have, Amy. But back then, when you started going out with Dan, we were both upset. We didn't want you throwing yourself away, and we worried."

"You had no right," Mom said angrily.

"Amy, stop it!" Dad said. "If your daughter started going out with a guy who had a criminal record and a reputation for being the wildest kid in town . . ."

"You were only a kid, Dan. Lots of kids are wild, and then she went ahead and—well—never mind."

"No," said Grandma Perl, "let's get it all out, and then maybe we can forget it ever happened. Somebody began stealing motorcycles in our neighborhood. Four of them, and I thought . . . maybe I wanted to think . . . it was your father. I thought I saw him."

"She called the police," Mom said, still angry. "She

told them she saw him, and they came and arrested him. That's when I told her I would never speak to her as long as I lived, and I ran away from home."

"We brought her back, but she kept running away, and we kept bringing her back. But when they found the thief who really stole the motorcycles, I guess we gave up. We knew there was no way to keep her home. She was never going to forgive us, and she absolutely refused to go away to college."

"Where did you go, Mom?" Ernest asked.

"I came here to San Francisco and lived with a friend of mine. I got a job as a receptionist for a dentist. Dad continued to work for a couple of years in that hardware store in Stockton, and he'd come up and see me weekends. Then he found a job here with Mr. Uhley, who used to own our store. That's when we got married."

"What a terrible story!" Gen shuddered. She couldn't think of anything that would ever make her run away from home and never see her parents again. She moved closer to Mom and leaned against her warm shoulder.

"I was wrong," Grandma said. "I knew I was wrong, but even knowing it isn't always enough to make a person change and do the right thing. But I was punished the most. I lost you for all those years, Amy, and . . . and I missed seeing the children as they grew up."

"Well," said Dad, "you came and you made this party

complete, Mrs. Perl. I know Amy has missed you. She's very stubborn, and I guess she's a little bit like you, too. She hates to admit when she's wrong."

"I wasn't wrong," Mom said.

"Yes, you were," Ernest said.

"Ernest!"

"Grandma did a bad thing accusing Dad of stealing the motorcycles, but she thought he did. And she was your mother and wanted to take care of you, even if she was wrong. Like Dad was wrong about me."

"He's some boy!" Grandma Perl said shakily. She put an arm out toward Mom, but Mom did not take it. "Amy—I brought you something. I baked you something you used to love."

She didn't have to say what it was, because suddenly Mom was all wrapped up in Grandma Perl, and everybody was laughing and crying except for Ernest, who unwrapped the package Grandma had brought, bent over it, sniffed it, and said, "It's a chocolate-chip cake, but it smells different."

CHAPTER TWENTY-TWO

It tasted different, too.

"Better!" Ernest said.

Worse, Gen thought, but she didn't want to hurt Grandma's feelings, so she kept her opinion to herself.

"What makes it taste different?" Ernest wanted to know.

"Ask your mother," Grandma told him, smiling mysteriously at Mom, as if only the two of them knew the secret ingredient.

But Mom looked puzzled. "Is there something different in it?" she asked. "I don't remember."

"I can't believe you forgot," Grandma said.

There were many cakes and pies and cookies at the party—a high, beautiful orange chiffon cake decorated with glazed oranges and fresh cherries; a coconut layer cake garnished with chocolate kisses; two strawberry pies with whipped cream; and a large, fancy vanilla lemon cake with HAPPY 25TH WEDDING ANNIVERSARY—AMY AND DAN written in silver letters across the top.

"I can't eat vanilla," Ernest confided to Grandma, helping himself to another piece of chocolate-chip cake.

"Why not?" Grandma wanted to know.

"It keeps me up at night," Ernest said.

"That's just stupid," Gen told him. "Chocolate keeps people up at night, not vanilla. And besides, the only thing that keeps you up at night is scary programs on TV that you're not supposed to watch."

Mom and Dad worked their way through the crowds of guests, introducing Grandma to just about everybody.

"I didn't know your mother lived in Stockton," Mrs. Ewing said.

"Oh, yes," said Mom, her arm around Grandma's shoulder as if they had been close all these twenty-five years. "That's where I grew up. And Dan, too."

"Well, you really do look alike," Wendy Knipper said. "But I think the one who looks most like you, Mrs. Perl, is Gen."

Gen looked at Grandma's old, wrinkled face and wondered how people could think she looked like an old woman who must be in her sixties at least.

Grandma didn't seem to mind. She smiled and said yes, everybody always said Amy looked just like her, and yes, she thought Gen did, too.

Grandma smiled and spoke comfortably with all her new acquaintances. She ate a plateful of food that Dad brought her and said everything was delicious. She acted as if Dad had cooked all the food, and she laughed at everything he said. Gen noticed that he stopped calling her Mrs. Perl and started calling her Adrienne.

Mom and Dad had to return to their other guests, and Grandma wandered around the house with Ernest and Gen. She said she thought the house was very nice, what she could see of it with so many people sitting and standing all over the place. "It's not usually this clean," Ernest told her. "Mom and Dad washed all the windows and even cleaned out the stove."

Grandma told them that she still lived in the same house Mom had grown up in. It was a big house, she said, with four bedrooms and a great big yard.

"Can we come out and visit you?" Ernest wanted to know.

"Of course you can," Grandma said. "I hope you'll all come, and stay over, too."

"Tell him he can't jump on the beds," Gen said. "He always breaks the beds when he stays over at Aunt Beth and Uncle Josh's."

"I don't *always* break their beds," Ernest defended himself.

Grandma told them there was still an old tree house that Mom used to play in when she was a girl. "I think it needs a lot of repairs," Grandma said, "and I'll try to have it fixed up for you before you come."

The party went on and on and on. Nobody made a move to go home. People were singing out on the deck, and then Mr. Ewing began dancing by himself downstairs in the garden.

"He's trampling the poppies," Gen told Karen.

"It's all right. We can always plant more," Karen said. "Let's go dance with him."

Gen did not feel like dancing, but most of her friends did. Andrea, Karen, and Jill, along with a bunch of happy grown-ups, joined the lone dancer.

Mrs. Ewing came out on the deck and looked down at her husband, arms upraised, stamping around in the middle of a large circle.

"He's never like this," she said stiffly to Gen. Then she called out, "Jim! Jim! You're making a fool of yourself. That's enough!"

"Oh—Bonnie!" Mr. Ewing called back. "I was looking all over for you. Come down, Bonnie, and dance with me."

"I don't think he was looking for me," said Mrs. Ewing.

"Bonnie! Bonnie!" yelled Mr. Ewing. "Come down and dance with me. Bonnie!"

Mrs. Ewing giggled. "Oh, well. It is a party, after all." She scurried downstairs as the guitar began playing:

Buffalo gals, won't you come out tonight
Come out tonight, come out tonight?
Buffalo gals, won't you come out tonight
And dance by the light of the moon?

There isn't any moonlight, Gen thought crabbily, looking up into the starry sky. She sat herself on one of the steps leading down to the garden. Mr. Robbins and Ms. Carrera hurried down the stairs, and Ms. Carrera said breathlessly as they passed her, "Gen, this is a wonderful party."

"The best party I've ever been to," said Mr. Robbins.

She watched them join the other dancers, and suddenly somebody yelled, "Amy and Dan! Amy and Dan! We want Amy and Dan!"

"I'll get them," her friend Andrea yelled, running up the stairs. "See," she said as she hurried past Gen, "I told you there was going to be dancing."

Soon Mom and Dad were down in the garden, dancing in the middle of a large circle of friends who clapped and cheered. Gen had never seen her parents dance, and she knew that Dad wasn't supposed to like dancing. But there the two of them were, jumping around and looking as if they were having a wonderful time. Dad was no longer wearing a tie, and his hair was messed up. Mom's shoes were off, and her makeup was smudged.

Ernest hurried past her. "Come on, Gen!" he said. "They're calling for us."

So she joined the circle, too, and then she and Ernest were pushed into the center, and people were clapping and cheering for them. Finally, even Grandma Perl ended up in the center with them, dancing with Ernest. Dad grabbed Gen's hand, and she and Dad and Mom danced together. When everybody began dancing with everybody else, Gen went back up the stairs as soon as she could and sat down in one corner of the deck.

"This is one great party," she heard somebody say.

And it was all she could do to keep herself from crying. She knew it was a great party, and she knew Mom and Dad were happy, and absolutely nothing had gone wrong. So, if the party was such a success, why was she feeling so miserable?

CHAPTER TWENTY-THREE

When Gen woke up early the following morning, the bad, heavy feeling was still there, deep, deep inside her. She looked over at Grandma Perl, fast asleep in the twin bed next to hers, and knew that she should be feeling happy. After more than twenty-five years, her grandmother and mother were reunited. Now she had a real grandmother who would make a fuss over her and buy her expensive presents as grandmothers were expected to do.

Very carefully, she eased herself out of bed and began tiptoeing out of the room. Grandma turned over but did not wake up. All was quiet in the upstairs hall. Everybody slept. The party had gone on and on until after two in the morning, and the smell of food still lingered. Very quietly, Gen moved downstairs and looked around her.

Everything was a mess. Nobody ever would have thought Mom and Dad had spent weeks cleaning up the place. There were paper cups, plates, and napkins every-where, and flecks of food dotted the carpet. Sticky baby hands had impressed themselves on the windows Mom and Dad had washed, and a broken bottle of sparkling cider still lay unswept in the hall.

Gen walked carefully around it into the equally dev-astated dining room. Splotches of food and drink stained the dining-room table and the floor. In the kitchen, dirty bowls and dishes were stacked in the sink, and the linoleum was stained and scuffed.

Gen opened the door to the deck and went outside. The deck was also a mess, with overturned chairs and crumpled papers everywhere.

The worst sight of all was the garden. Gen sat down on the top step and looked at the trampled flowers and rutted earth. The dancing had destroyed all of the pretty wildflowers; except for the little rock garden over near the fence, nothing remained of all the weeks and weeks of hard work.

But there was something else inside her that was hurting. More than the gigantic cleanup that lay ahead, there was something else that hurt even more.

"Gen?"

Mom came out on the deck and said sleepily, "You're up early. It's only eight."

"I couldn't sleep," Gen said.

Mom moaned. "I need a cup of coffee. I'll be right back."

Gen could hear kitchen sounds, and finally she smelled coffee. Mom came back and sat down next to her, holding a cup.

"What a party!" she said. "Oh, my head!"

She sipped her coffee and then sighed, "The place is a total mess. I always tell your father, never clean before a party. The time to clean is afterward."

"You weren't surprised," Gen said, "were you?"

Mom hesitated.

"Come on, Mom. I know you weren't surprised. You never would have cleaned the house if you were."

"You've got me there," Mom admitted. "But, of course, we were very surprised when we first realized you were planning a party."

"It was that Wendy Knipper, wasn't it?" Gen said bitterly. "I knew she was the one."

"No, as a matter of fact, it was Uncle Josh. But don't tell him I told you." Mom began to laugh. "He kept calling and calling to remind us that he was going to pick us up at six sharp and to remind us not to be late. Dad suggested finally that maybe we should make it at seven, and then Josh said there wouldn't be enough time if we made it at seven. That's when we figured it out."

"I wanted it to be a surprise," Gen said. "I really wanted it to be a surprise."

Mom put down her cup and laid an arm on Gen's shoulder. "It was a surprise, Gen, an amazing surprise. All those people—I'm not even sure we knew them all."

"That's just it. I wanted it to be a small surprise party with people you knew, but everybody else got involved, and nobody cared what I wanted."

Mom pulled Gen over to her. "It was a wonderful party, Gen, and it was your idea in the beginning. And the best part of it—really—the absolute best thing was . . ."

"I know," Gen said. "It was bringing Grandma here."

"Yes, darling, that was the best. I have my mother back again, thanks to you and Ernest."

"It was Ernest," Gen said between her teeth. "He was the one who invited her. He was the one who sent her the bus fare, even though she drove. Everybody thinks he's so great, and he is. It was his idea. He's changed. He's a different person. He's a good person, and I hate him."

"You don't have to hate him," Mom said, "and I'm not so sure he's changed that much."

"Well, it was his idea to invite Grandma to the party. He was the one who invited her. Not me."

"But you were the one who thought up the party in the first place, weren't you?"

"I guess so, but it didn't turn out the way I planned."

"But look at everything that did happen because you thought up the idea."

"What?" Gen asked, allowing Mom to draw her even closer.

"Look at all the people who got involved—who wanted to get involved. Look at all the new friends Dad and I have made, and you too, Gen. And business has even improved in the store, I think because of the party."

"What else?" Gen asked, snuggling deeper into Mom's side as the miserable feeling began to ease.

"You made Dad and me very happy. I can't tell you how wonderful it is to have a daughter like you who worked so hard to give us such a good time."

"Ernest helped, too," Gen muttered.

"Well, yes, he did. And wasn't it wonderful for a change that he wanted to help, and do something so thoughtful? And isn't it good that he made Grandma happy? He never would have thought of it if you hadn't planned the surprise party."

"What else?" Gen felt the sun on her head.

"Well, everybody had such a good time, even—" Mom giggled "—even Ms. Carrera and Mr. Robbins. You know, Gen, I really do think we may have a budding romance on our hands because of the party. And look at

Wendy Knipper and Karen. Suddenly they're really getting along—thanks to the party."

Ernest came out onto the deck. "I know what the secret ingredient is," he said.

"Ernest," Mom said, "you didn't wake up Grandma, did you?"

"No, she was up, making her bed. Dad's the only one who's still sleeping. Anyway, I know what the secret ingredient is."

"What?" Gen asked, lifting her head up from Mom's shoulder.

"A mashed banana," Ernest announced.

"Yuk! I hate mashed bananas." Gen shuddered.

"Well, she's going to make another one today just for the family. There's none left from yesterday."

"I won't eat it," Gen said. "I'll make my own."

Ernest looked over her head down at the garden. "Hey," he said, "the yard looks the way it used to look."

"It's terrible, isn't it," Gen said. "But maybe we can clean it up and plant some more wildflower seeds."

"No, I don't want to," Ernest said, running down the stairs. "It was too much work. It wasn't any fun except watering it when you were around, Gen. I couldn't have water fights with my friends, and we couldn't dig holes."

"Mom!"

"Oh, dear!" Mom said feebly. "I guess we could try to plant a lawn."

"I don't want a lawn," Ernest yelled. "I want it the way it used to be."

"Well, I don't," Gen said, also moving down the stairs, and facing Ernest. "You always get your way, you brat!"

"You're the brat," Ernest retorted.

"Listen, kids, I have an idea," Mom said, coming down the stairs. "How about sharing the yard?"

"Garden," Gen corrected.

"Yard," Ernest insisted.

"Okay! Okay! It can be both. Look, Gen, your rock garden looks great, and there's lots of room around the back there near the fence if you want to expand it. Ernest can play in the front of the yard, and you'll have the back."

"I'd have to put up barbed wire," Gen said, "or he'll get into it. He gets into everything."

"I'll water it for you," Ernest offered, the mean smile spreading across his face. "I'll go get the hose right now. Just stay right there."

Gen reached out and grabbed him. While he struggled, the bad feeling completely left her. In spite of all the changes, some things, she realized, would never change.

DISCARDED
Goshen Public Library

Grandma Perl's Easy Chocolate-Chip Cake

■ ■ ■ ■ ■

You'll need:
  2 cups flour
  1 cup sugar
  $\frac{1}{2}$ cup (1 stick) butter or margarine
  $\frac{1}{2}$ teaspoon baking powder
  1 egg
  1 cup sour milk or buttermilk or yogurt
  1 teaspoon baking soda
  1 teaspoon vanilla extract
  6 ounces semisweet chocolate chips
  $\frac{1}{2}$ or 1 small banana (optional)

With a pastry blender or two knives, blend together 2 cups flour, 1 cup sugar, and a bar of butter or margarine until coarse crumbs form. Remove $\frac{2}{3}$ cup and save for the topping.

Sprinkle $\frac{1}{2}$ teaspoon baking powder over mixture, and add one beaten egg. Set aside.

Meanwhile, have 1 cup of sour milk ready. (To make sour milk, just add 1 scant tablespoon of vinegar to 1 cup of milk and allow to sit for five minutes or more. If this sounds like too much work, you can substitute 1 cup of buttermilk or yogurt.) Dissolve 1 teaspoon baking soda in milk mixed with 1 teaspoon vanilla. Add milk all at once to flour mixture, and stir only until liquid is completely absorbed. Add 6 ounces semisweet chocolate chips, and stir.

Pour into either a greased 8" square pan (for a higher, lighter cake) or a 9" square pan (for a lower, heavier cake, but it looks like more). Sprinkle reserved topping over batter. Bake in a 350° oven until cake springs back when pressed. It will take about 45–50 minutes for an 8" cake, 35–40 minutes for a 9" cake.

P.S. If you agree with Ernest, you can add ½ or 1 small mashed banana after blending in the liquid. If you agree with Gen, don't.

J
SAC

Sachs, Marilyn.
Surprise party

W

7SOL

AR 4.4   4PtS